Montgomery M. Folsom

Scraps of Song and Southern Scenes

A Collection of Humorous and Pathetic Poems and Descriptive Sketches

Montgomery M. Folsom

Scraps of Song and Southern Scenes
A Collection of Humorous and Pathetic Poems and Descriptive Sketches

ISBN/EAN: 9783337181277

Printed in Europe, USA, Canada, Australia, Japan

Cover: Foto ©Andreas Hilbeck / pixelio.de

More available books at **www.hansebooks.com**

SCRAPS OF SONG

AND

SOUTHERN SCENES

BY

MONTGOMERY M. FOLSOM

A Collection of

HUMOROUS AND PATHETIC POEMS AND DESCRIP-
TIVE SKETCHES OF PLANTATION LIFE IN
THE BACKWOODS OF GEORGIA.

ATLANTA, GEORGIA:
CHAS. P. BYRD, PUBLISHER
1889

Faithfully
Montgomery M. Folsom.

TABLE OF CONTENTS.

PREFACE.

In placing before the public this little volume, I feel that I am appealing to an audience whose sympathies are already mine. Yet, if the full measure of my anticipations be not wholly realized, I shall still feel that the world has been so kind and generous to me, that I can well afford to submit uncomplainingly to a light reproof now and then.

Should these little emanations of my intellect meet with favor in the eyes of those for whose pleasure they are written, and should they touch a responsive chord in the hearts of those among whom my life has been passed, and to whom every sympathy of my soul goes out in fond endearment; then shall I feel that I have not written in vain of the melody and memory of my old plantation home.

MONTGOMERY M. FOLSOM.

DEDICATION.

To HENRY W. GRADY.

TRUE FRIEND:

> *To whom my heart hath turned*
> *When in Life's skies in splendor burned*
> *The Star of Hope. And oft to whom*
> *My soul hath looked when deepest gloom*
> *Of dark adversity appalled:*

TO THEE:

> *To whom I oft have called,*
> *For help and sympathy and cheer*
> *When clouds were dark and skies were drear,*
> *And never, never, called in vain;*
> *This modest tribute of my brain*

IN LOVE

> *I dedicate, and bring*
> *With this a heart's free offering,*
> *Through every change or varying mood,*
> *Of deep, undying gratitude.*

THE AUTHOR.

SCRAPS OF SONG.

ST. AUGUSTINE.

A city built upon the sands
St. Augustine, the Ancient, stands.
Eastward, the black Matanzas' wave;
Westward, Sebastian's waters lave
The marshes stretching toward the main ·
Landward, a waste of barren plain.
So grim, so gray, and old, it seems
A realm of half-remembered dreams.

Where rose her walls there's scarce a clod,
Aspires above the levelled sod;
Where trails and clambers, wild and free,
The fragrant rose of Cherokee;
And clumps of stunted cedars grow;
Gnarled willows in the moat below
Whose depth now measures scarce a span,
Shallow as the vaunt of boasting man!

Twin shafts of crumbling brick and stone,
The ancient gateway stands alone;
Around those once commanding towers;
Now cling the golden jasmine flowers;
While through yon great breach, yawning wide,
Oozes a stream whose listless tide,
Emboldened by the sad decay,
Unchallenged winds its sluggish way.

Fair even in age the Plaza gay,
Where fountains shower their crystal spray,
And wreaths of odorous orange bloom
Burden the air with rich perfume,
And whispering south winds sway and toss

The long festoons of sombre moss.
In shaded nooks where sunbeams play
At hide-and-seek, the livelong day.

But blackened ruins mark the spot—
On this fair scene the only blot—
Where once the old slave market stood
When trafficked men in human blood,
And Afric's sons were bought and sold
Like sheep and swine for Spanish gold ;
And rude Oppression forced apart
The tenderest ties that bind the heart !

Down by the placid river's marge,
Where sloop and schooner, bark and barge,
And gilded yacht at anchor lie,
And white-winged gulls are circling high;
Seaward the current sets, and fast
The ebbing tide goes rushing past;
The waves along the old sea wall,
In rythmic cadence, rise and fall.

With awe and reverence strong and deep,
I mount that castellated steep,
Beneath whose portals, roughly arched,
The mail-clad Spaniard proudly marched,
While boom of thunderous cannon rolled,
And storms of martial music told
That Spain's broad banner still unfurled
It's conquering folds o'er half the world !

The mitred abbot chanted here
The glad Te Deum, loud and clear,
And St. Iago's name was praised
While trumpets rang and bonfires blazed.
Within this court yard's ample space
Proud Valor paid to Beauty's grace,
On bended knee, the homage due
From loyal knight to lady true.

Above yon rugged arch I trace
Lines that all time can ne'er efface—
Deep graven in the dark grey stone
The royal seal of Arragon!
And just below the graver wrote
A name that like a bugle note
Stirred many a heart, nerved many a hand,
The kingly name of Ferdinand!

Deserted now each vaulted room
And voiceless is the donjon's gloom.
My footsteps in the lonely keep
Disturb the hermit echoes' sleep.
Th' "Alerta!" of the sentinel
Is heard no more; the castle bell
Is hushed; and 'neath the turret's crest
A brooding screech owl builds her nest.

Within that tower I sit and gaze
To'ard the dull bank of purple haze
Where earth and sky and ocean meet,
And wild Atlantic billows beat
Upon the bar, where ghastly white
The sand dunes glisten in the light,
Like some dead isle's gaunt skeleton
Left bleaching, crumbling, in the sun.

But day is dying! Swift and fleet
The twilight speeds with flying feet,
While Anastasia's shores grow dim
Old Ocean chants his Vesper hymn.
A widowed seabird sadly croons
Her dismal lay among the dunes.
A thousand stars in silvery sheen
Look down on old St. Augustine

ALMOST HOME.

Last Words of Hon. Benjamin Harvey Hill.

Where moaning rolls the troubled wave,
Whose tempest-tortured waters lave
Life's furthest shore, his spirit stands,
Half pausing on the crumbling sands.
Exultant words in triumph wrung
In joy from that long silent tongue,
He looks beyond the tossing foam,
And sweetly murmurs, " Almost home!"

No more with woe and weakness cursed—
Disease and death have done their worst;
The dream of life is left behind,
Though near are hearts whose chords are twined
Around his own. Forgetful quite,
His kindling eye reflects the light
Resplendent from the radiant dome
Of heaven. He whispers "Almost home!"

All heedless of the winds that wail
Along the lone and shadowy vale,
And recking not the storms that sweep
The desert strand, or eyes that weep
Salt dews in bitterest anguish shed,
Blent with the death-damps on his head.
Hark! Softly through the gathering gloom
The tremulous accents, "Almost home!"

As when among the shivering leaves
The parting sigh of autumn grieves,
So comes the plaintive, shuddering gasp,
And snaps in twain the golden clasp.
The boatman plies his muffled oar,
The bark glides swiftly from the shore.
And from the faltering lips there come
The dying echoes, "Almost home!"

No more with pain or passion blind,
That kingly spirit, unconfined
By earthly fetters, bolts or bars,
Victorious mounts beyond the stars ;
And wings its flight with undimmed eyes
Across the plains of Paradise,
In freedom evermore to roam—
Not almost now, but quite " at home ! "

WE MEET NO MORE.

We meet no more ! In separate ways
  Our feet must walk alone,
With haunting thoughts of happier days
  And pleasures past and gone.
Borne earthward by relentless fate
  Whenever our hopes would soar,
For the light that came, came all too late,
  And we shall meet no more !

We meet no more ! Our longing eyes
  Forever backward turned
To that dull dreary waste that lies
  Where once love's beacon burned ;
Among the shadows wan and murk
  That shroud the dismal shore,
Not even the ghosts of gladness walk,
  For we shall meet no more !

We meet no more ! The stars are dim,
  The night winds grieve and moan ;
Along the far horizon's rim
  The hills, now bleak and lone,
Recall the wildest, sweetest dream
  That ever a summer bore ;
But of all its light no lingering beam,
  For we shall meet no more !

We meet no more ! The radiant past
  Intensifies the gloom,
As sorrow's twilight shadows fast

Darken to deeper doom !
I call your dear name once again,
   As oft I've done before,
And my heart echoes the sad refrain
   That we shall meet no more !

We meet no more !   Each tender look,
   Each smile since first you came,
Each golden page in memory's book
   Contains your sacred name !
Each scribbled note you wrote me, and
   A bunch of flowers you wore,
Dearer than men can understand,
   Since we shall meet no more !

We meet no more !   O say it not,
   But grant me this last prayer,
That all the past may be forgot,
   And you will meet me there
At the old tryst, with radiant face,
   Love-litten as of yore :
Ah, 'tis but a phantom hope I chase,
   For we shall meet no more !

We meet no more !   The sun may shine
   In April's fairest skies,
And make the glorious earth divine
   With summer's changing dyes ;
The birds may sing in leafy woods,
   When winter's storms are o'er,
While this sad soul in silence broods
   That we shall meet no more !

We meet no more !   My life, my love,
   It is so hard to bear !
In earth, nor sea, nor heavens above,
   There's none my grief to share,
And not a joy this world can give
   To cheer this bosom's core.
For I've nothing left for which to live,
   Since we shall meet no more !

RARE PINK WILD ROSE.

Rare pink wild rose!
When April's tender cheek first glows
With the warm kisses of the sun,
A fond caress she fain would shun;
Yet with a maiden's witching wiles
Looks upward thro' her tears, and smiles;
Then by the budding hedgerow blows
    The pink wild rose.

Fair pink wild rose!
How sweet the day when earth first throws
Aside her mantle and unfolds
Her robes of green, and one beholds
The wreaths of silvery mists that float
And twine about her slender throat,
Where, mingled with her blushes, shows
    A wild pink rose!

Ah! pink wild rose!
Although thy cultured sister grows
Where wealth, refinement, every care
Conspire to render her most fair;
Yet there's a charm about thee still
That all the patient gardener's skill
Can ne'er attain, as well he knows—
    Thou pink wild rose!

Sweet pink wild rose!
A soft and subtle fragrance flows
From thy pale petals. Oft it seems
A touch of half-forgotten dreams,
That bring to earth the chastened dyes
And pure perfumes of Paradise.
Kind heaven a precious boon bestows
    In thee, wild rose!

HOUNDED DOWN.

"We are sorry, indeed, for the widow,"
  Say the law-loving men of the town;
You are sorry, indeed, for the widow,
The bereaved one who sits in the shadow,
While sunshine floods wood, field and meadow—
  You that hounded him down!

Yes, his sorrow was of his own entailing,
  But not of such heinous renown,
That you all should keep railing and railing,
When you saw that his body was ailing,
And you knew that his spirit was failing—
  You that hounded him down!

Who are you, that the sinner should tremble,
  And quake at your virtuous frown?
With your proud pharisaical amble,
And your shrewd hypocritical shamble,
Who have taught your own hearts to dissemble—
  You that hounded him down?

Were you each a ringmaster of heaven,
  And he but a pitiful clown?
Were your souls by particular leaven
Made perfect—-your sins all forgiven?
He alone left a sinner unshriven—
  You that hounded him down?

God knows which of you will inherit
  The stars and the glittering crown;
And whether the martyr's meek spirit,
Or the strong-hearted hero will merit—
Whether he will deserve most to wear it,
  Or you that hounded him down!

BEYOND THE MOUNTAIN.

Beyond the mountain's rugged crest,
    A pleasant valley lieth;
A country blessed with peace and rest,
Beyond the glorious, golden west,
    Where pleasure never dieth;
Through green fields spreading far and wide,
    Floweth a shining river,
And side by side, upon that tide,
Our soul-ships shall at anchor ride,
    Forever and forever!

Beyond the mountain cold and gray,
    The sun is ever shining,
Where softly play the lights of May,
Through all the calm and dreamful day
    No shadow or declining;
And we shall dwell where roses grow
    With odorous dews aquiver,
And violets blow, bright waters flow,
And west winds whisper sweet and low
    Forever and forever!

Beyond the mountain brown and bleak,
    Shall burst upon our vision
The sunlit peak and crystal creek,
And all the beauteous scenes that speak
    The poet-soul's elysian;
There shall we feel and understand—
    Suffering and fearing never,
But blithe and bland in that fair land,
Where we shall wander hand in hand
    Forever and forever!

Beyond the mountain mists that shroud
    The sunset's radiant splendor,
Hearts shall be bowed beneath a cloud
Of sin no more, but heaven-endowed
    With feelings true and tender,
Aroused from earth's wild troubled dream,
    And life's short, fitful fever,
Each living stream will catch the gleam
Of sacred truth's undying beam,
    Forever and forever!

Beyond the mountain dark and grim
    No angry storms shall gather ;
No cloud shall dim the golden rim
Of life's rich cup filled to the brim
    With endless summer weather.
No more the autumn winds shall wail,
    Nor bare trees sigh and shiver ;
Each laden gale that sweeps the vale
Shall breathe anew love's tenderest tale
    Forever and forever!

Beyond the mountain grave and stern,
    Forgotten life's sad story
Of hearts that burn and grieve and yearn
For joys that nevermore return,
    And youth's departed glory!
Beyond the pale of mortal woe,
    Naught shall our spirits sever,
To loftier tone our spirits grown
With purer joys than earth hath known,
    Forever and forever!

CHRISTMAS CAROL.

From the dark, snow-bound solitudes
Of lonely Lapland's wintry woods,
O'er ice-bound hill and frosty plain,
The King of Christmas guides his train.
Southward, ho! he swiftly speeds,
Driven by six fleet-footed steeds,
And pausing not, he dare not stay,
He has too many calls to pay.
    Busy, too, his treasures summing,
    Old Santa Claus is coming,
    Coming, coming, coming, coming,
    Santa Claus is coming, coming,
    He is right now on the way!

By frozen lake and sleety stream,
And wind-swept wastes that shivering gleam
In the twilight of the sickly noon,
Or wan rays of the widowed moon;
From mystic regions cold and drear,
Where beetling crags of ice uprear
Bleak brows to meet the sunless day
Along the shores of Baffin bay,
    With its foam-capped billows booming,
    Old Santa Claus is coming,
    Coming, coming, coming, coming,
    Santa Claus is coming, coming,
    He is right now on the way!

By lordly hall and princely dome,
By many an humble cottage home:
Through restless city spreading wide,
Through quiet, cosy country side;
Beneath December's glittering stars
That peep through midnight's ebon bars:
Through forest paths where sprite and fay,
Wood nymphs and fairies are at play:

2

In the tender twilight gloaming,
Old Santa Claus is coming,
Coming, coming, coming, coming.
Santa Claus is coming, coming,
He is right now on the way !

Ah! many a childish heart is light,
And many a childish eye is bright,
And many a childish pulse beats fast
With every wail that wings the blast;
As sinks the sunset's fading rim
Beyond the distant mountain's dim;
And older hearts far backward stray,
Age is forgot and youth holds sway.
    Once more their heart strings thrumming,
    Old Santa Claus is coming,
    Coming, coming, coming, coming,
    Santa Claus is coming, coming.
    He is right now on the way!

Hark! upon the crisp night air
Sound the revels loud and clear,
Awakened by the festive throng,
Boist'rous laugh, discordant song,
With startling clash and clamorous din,
The wondrous Day is ushered in;
And myriad tongues in glad array
Chant the anthems blithe and gay.
    The deep-toned bells are drumming,
    For Santa Claus is coming,
    Coming, coming, coming, coming,
    Santa Claus is coming, coming,
    He is right now on the way!

O'er field and wood and frosty lea,
Along the dark, remorseful sea,
In Mirth's unloosed, abandon sweep.
Around the world, from steep to steep,

And bid the riotous echoes fly
From shadowy earth to arching sky,
From mist-robed mountains, grim and gray,
Up to the star-gemmed Milky Way;
    Send the echoes, throbbing, humming,
    Old Santa Claus is coming,
    Coming, coming, coming, coming,
    Santa Claus is coming, coming,
    He is right now on the way!

IS IT WRONG?

    Is it wrong
To love you madly, and to long
For your dear presence every hour
With all the concentrated power
And strength of heart and mind and soul,
When even the dream-bells toll and toll
The echoes of your sacred name?
If it be wrong, I'll bear the blame
Of all these wild desires that throng
My heart, if it be wrong.

    Is it wrong
To drift in loneliness along
The tide of life, and dream of lands
Beyond the stars, where these weak hands
Shall clasp thine own in warm embrace?
And, gazing in thy radiant face,
I shall read more than boasts the lore
Of all the ages gone before,
And weave your being in the song
That fills my heaven—Ah, is it wrong?

CUMBERLAND.

Oh, Cumberland, sweet Cumberland,
   Thou placid land of summer calms,
Love-dream of summery slumberland,
   Where chant the waves their softest psalms;
In thy sun-burnished panoply
   The gentlest winds around thee sweep.
Beneath heaven's azure canopy,
   The silvery circlet of the deep.

The long, low stretch of mottled sands,
   The spectral dunes that guard the beach,
The hungering billows—boisterous bands
   Of bold marauders—upward reach
To break thy barriers, and to claim
   Thee for their captive queen once more;
And each hath carved his barbarous name
   In hieroglyphics on the shore.

Among thy woodlands, twilight dim,
   The shrouded ghosts of history glide,
Breathing some legendary hymn
   Through grey salt marshes spreading wide,
Where sombre mantled cedars brood,
   And listlessly repeat again
To whispering reeds, in tones subdued,
   The wild hexameters of the main.

And Dungeness, grim Dungeness—
   Gray memory of a golden dream—
Where medieval loveliness,
   With modern luxury, is the theme;
Plantation days are vanished, but
   Among yon brambly sedges gleam
The walls of many a crumbling hut—
   Reminders of the old regime.

A lowly mound where sleeps some slave
    In hearing of the restful sea;
Hardby the stone that marks the grave
    Of gallant Lighthorse Harry Lee!
The bondsman's chain is broken now,
    His labor and his longings o'er;
Around the chieftain's laureled brow
    The storm of battle bursts no more.

In contemplative attitude   .
    The moss-draped oaks stand silent there—
Veiled sisters of the cloistered wood,
    With reverent heads low bowed in prayer;
And many a soft " Our Father " sighs,
    And low " Hail Mary," sad and sweet
As some faint waifling zephyr, dies
    Among the violets at their feet.

EDGAR ALLAN POE.

Proud genius scales the mountain height,
    Slow drudgery plods the vale ;
In the blaze of a single meteor bright,
    A hundred planets pale.
To thee immortal glory given
    Above life's careworn crowds,
Far as the glittering stars of heaven
    Are above the drifting clouds.

Thou wert no child of bondage, Poe,
    But born to love the sun,
With a high contempt for earth's vain show
    And its empty triumphs won.
Better the free wild flowers should twine
    'Round thy neglected grave,
Than thou shouldst fill the gilded shrine
    Of an earth-bound, soulless slave.

So touchingly sweet the wild refrains
  That from thy soul upwell,
They rival the rare, melodious strains
  Of that angel Israfel,
Doomed by a fateful destiny
  Like thine to soothe each smart.
With chords of such grief-born melody
  As filled thy desolate heart.

Through heaven's far sun-gilt solitudes,
  The kingly eagle sweeps;
In the haunted depths of the sombre woods,
  The craven screech-owl sleeps;
One soars aloft to meet his foes,
  In the broad, bright beams of day.
The other steals forth at evening's close
  To murder his weakling prey.

Misunderstood and oft misjudged,
  Poor victim of despair,
Malice denied and envy grudged
  The fame they could not share;
And even amid death's solemn gloom,
  Insatiate vultures vile,
They gathered about that sacred tomb
  To desecrate and defile.

When honest critics' tongues were mute,
  Because they could not wake
The music from that broken lute,
  These ghouls e'en dared to break
The spell of thine undying fame,
  With calumnies so black
Posterity hides its face in shame
  And hurls the falsehoods back.

LOVER'S OAK—BRUNSWICK.

There's many an oak in Brunswick wood,
    And many a stalwart pine.
In solemn, stately attitude
The dark, majestic cedars brood;
    Hardby the sobbing brine.

But in this woodland's deepest nook,
    All scarred and seamed with age,
Uprears an oak of lordly look
Whose smallest branch might safely brook
    The cyclone's wildest rage.

Down from its boughs the gray moss creeps
    Like beard of patriarch hoar,
Each fluttering lock that earthward leaps
Marks well the line its circle sweeps
    A hundred feet or more.

A thousand times the vernal sun
    Hath warmed its sluggish veins ;
Ten ages burned the summer noon,
Ten centuries hath fallen the swoon
    Of chill November rains.

Full many a tale this ancient tree
    Could, if it would, impart !
And many a tender history
Of budding love's dear mystery,
    Locked in its rugged heart.

'Twas here, ere Art at Nature scoffed,
    Or history had a name,
At twilight's sacred season oft,
With airy footsteps, swift and soft,
    The Indian maiden came.

The plumed and painted warrior brought
    The trophies of the chase ;
Knelt at her feet and there besought—
His soul with love's sweet madness fraught—
    The comfort of her grace.

Here came the proud Castilian maid,
    Whose languorous, melting eyes,
Like twinkling stars illumed the glade,
Half hopeful and yet half afraid,
    She watched the purpling skies.

Her fiery lover fiercely pressed,
    In whispers deep and low,
His suit—the story long suppressed—
While died far down the darkling west
    The sunset's fading glow.

And when the ambient evening air
    In fragrant freshness blew,
The Anglo-Saxon lass, so fair,
Came, with her lustrous, golden hair,
    And eyes of summer hue.

And, like some frightened forest bird,
    She fluttered in this bower;
And in love's tenderest accents heard
The same sweet tale, and drank each word
    That blessed that holy hour.

And still the youth of Brunswick seek
    This ancient tryst to spell
Affection's spotless page, and speak
To listening ears and flushing cheek
    The tale so hard to tell.

Till Providence completes the sum
    Of days that time shall be ;

Until creation's voice grows dumb;
Through all the years they still will come
    To this old trysting tree.

There's many a tree in Brunswick wood,
    Whose leaves the sea-winds kiss;
But none can touch the poet's mood
And furnish fancy such rare food
    For golden dreams as this.

THE DISAPPOINTED.

A conquerer forced to act the clown,
    Some vague experiment of fate,
With every grief to drag me down,
    Though every gift to make me great;
I've searched the world for happiness,
    A wanderer over land and sea;
And learned, alas! the joys that bless
    For others are and not for me!

A soul so sensitive that all
    My lesser woes are magnified;
I crouch beneath a shadowy pall
    Of dumb remorse and sullen pride;
Walled in with weaknesses that crush
    Each hope of what I long to be;
I cannot weep. I will not blush,
    Knowing these hopes are not for me.

This willful heart, unreasoning, blind,
    Hath cherished many a fond desire,
Trusting that gold of truth, refined
    By erring passion's fiercest fire,
Might purchase peace and sweet content;
    But destiny rejects the fee,
And leaves my longing and regret
    That dreams like these are not for me!

LADY MINE.

A VALENTINE.

As I kneel before the shrine,
Of the good saint. Lady mine,
I will breathe an humble prayer
That I once again may share
Those sweet hours that once we knew
When the violets drank the dew,
    And I was your valentine,
        Lady mine!

Do not chide me, lady mine,
If by word and look and sign
I the secret sweet reveal
That my heart would fain conceal :
And the world the secret learns
Through the blazing fire that burns
' In my soul like new made wine.
        Lady mine!

Here beside the surging brine
I am wandering, lady mine;
Where the wild, grey billows roll,
Emblems of this restless soul !
Where the storms of passion rave
As tempests lash the windswept wave,
    Thoughts the earth cannot confine,
        Lady mine!

Lulls the gale. 'Mid scenes divine
I am dreaming, lady mine.
Vagrantly my footsteps stray
Through the woodlands far away :
In spirit now I hold thy hand
On the lone shores of Cumberland,
    Watching daylight's slow decline,
        Lady mine!

Radiant stars in skies benign
Rise above me, lady mine:
Swiftly from the distant deep,
Wraithlike sea mists stealthily creep.
Widowed spirits of the main
Doomed to haunt the shores in vain—
   Doomed in sadness to repine,
       Lady mine!

Upon the far horizon line
The young moon trembles, lady mine:
Down dim vistas, far remote,
Golden clouds at anchor float;
Half in sky and half in sea,
Freighted dreamships, drifting free.
   Where the hope stars brightest shine,
       Lady mine!

Here the trailing jasmine vine
Buds and blossoms, lady mine;
Here the dark magnolia trees,
Stirred by the sensuous ocean breeze,
Whisper words of life and hope;
While on a violet scented slope,
   In listless languor, I recline,
       Lady mine!

All these joys would I resign
For thy presence, lady mine;
With those love-illumined eyes,
Brighter than Brunswick's bluest skies;
And to make the dream complete—
Those soft accents low and sweet,
   Then would life its charms combine,
       Lady mine!

Let thine arms around me twine,
Smile and kiss me, lady mine—
As the laughing breakers kiss

The summer shore, and, drunk with bliss,
Reel backward, turn and upward leap
Along the yielding shores, and sweep
Its heaving bosom snowy fair,
With their shining, golden hair—
   For I am thine, forever thine,
      Lady mine!

SHE SWEETLY SLEEPS.

   She sweetly sleeps!
Night wind that grieves and sweeps
Along the dark, deserted streets,
While Nature's heart in pity beats
O'er sins and sorrows of the day,
And those whose erring footsteps stray.
Beset with perils, passion blind,
Through ways and woes of human kind:
Oh, wind, no need that wailing, thou
Disturb that calm and placid brow;
For there around that precious head
The dews of sinless sleep are shed;
The restful zephyr softly creeps,
   She sweetly sleeps!

   She sweetly sleeps!
Unmindful of the heart that weeps
In loneliness and longing drear
For light that will no more appear
Above life's far horizon line,
And paint the world in hues divine,
Of soft blue skies and golden gleams,
September dies and Summer dreams!
Yet, whisper in her ear, oh, gale!
The burden of a tender tale
That I would tell, were I the sprite
That shaped her visions of the night,
While bound in gentle slumber's deeps.
   She sweetly sleeps!

SLEEP ON!

IN MEMORY OF MISS JESSIE HARDEMAN.

Sleep on, sleep on, fair mortal;
   Sweet shall thy slumber be;
Beyond Life's closing portal
   No dreams shall trouble thee.

Sleep on! Thy calm, cool pillow
   Supports a painless brow;
Time's farthest-reaching billow
   Shall ne'er disturb thee now.

The sun shall shine above thee,
   The moon shall rise and wane;
The summer winds that love thee
   Shall lisp thy name in vain;

And miss the songs of gladness
   That silent voice hath sung;
Night dews shall weep in sadness
   For one who died so young!

But, oh, a wondrous story
   Those mystic voices croon—
They tell of brighter glory
   Than gilds the skies of June.

Of songs whose grander measure
   In rythmic stanzas flow;
And strains of purer pleasure
   Than earth can ever know.

Sleep on, sleep on, fair mortal;
   Thy waking eyes shall see
Beyond Life's closing portal
   Heaven's blest eternity.

A RETROSPECT.

Sweet promise! But thy broken bow
　　Half spans the dreary lea;
The wild despairing gales that blow
My heart's despondent throbs echo.
Dear love! Ah! you will never know
　　What you have been to me!

The tiresome years will drag along
　　In dull monotony:
I mingle with the weary throng
That my poor lot is cast among,
With this the burden of my song—
　　What you have been to me!

The time will come in after years,
　　As the remorseful sea
Gives up at last the dead it bears—
When retrospective sorrow sears
Your soul, you'll wonder through your tears
　　What you have been to me!

Love grieves and, grudging, views the flight
　　Of hours that swiftly flee
Through days that bring no more delight,
Through the long watches of the night,
And memory mourns the life and light
　　That you have been to me!

'Tis many a day since gladly beat
　　My heart from sorrow free;
The tripping of your dainty feet;
Your gentle voice, each new conceit,
To others but a trifle, sweet,
　　But all the world to me!

And oh, how I have madly prayed
  To heaven that I might be—
With all my pain and passion stayed,
Through morn and noon and twilight shade,
In some new gift and guise arrayed—
  What you have been to me!

A SPRAY OF HELIOTROPE.

A withered spray of heliotrope,
  With one poor faded blossom,
Fit emblem of a cherished hope
  Borne in this restless bosom.

Were't like that " Resurrection Rose,"
  In Mexic legend tender,
That 'neath the showers of April blows
  Anew in heightened splendor;

So might that dead hope bloom again,
  In beauteous form and fashion,
After the driving, blinding rain
  Of some wild gust of passion.

Reminder of what I would forget—
  The glamor and the glory,
The sacred joy, the vain regret
  Of one sweet summer story.

Though shadows dark increase the scope
  Of sorrows that enslave me,
I'll keep this spray of heliotrope
  That long ago you gave me!

CLARIBEL!

Claribel, Claribel!
Do you know adown the dell
Where Love's ministering spirits dwell,
        Dearest one:
Trills the June gale's welcome note;
Shines the humming bird afloat,
Like a flashing, golden mote
        In the sun.

Claribel, Claribel!
Shadows lengthen, and the swell
Of the nightwind sounds the knell
        Of the day:
'Neath a pall of purple cloud,
Mists of amber for his shroud,
Lies in state its monarch proud,
        Far away!

Claribel, Claribel!
Will you listen while I tell
That old story conned so well,
        While afar
Glows the twilight with the mirth
That illumines all the earth,
And the heavens o'er the birth
        Of a star!

Claribel, Claribel!
Ah! the glamor and the spell
Of rare odors and the smell
        Of the musk;
Droops each dewy blossomed stalk
Just to listen to you talk,
As with dallying feet we walk
        In the dusk!

'Claribel, Claribel!
Not for years of asphodel
Bordered Eden would I sell
One sweet hour
Of enjoyment such as this,
With the burden and the bliss
Of my lady's tender kiss
In her bower!

AFTER-THOUGHTS.

Once more I clasp that soft white hand
In mine: Again my cheek is fanned
By that pure breath whose faintest swell
Pulsates a heart that loves me well.

Once more the love notes ebb and flow
Like murmurous May-winds, sweet and low,
And in those soul-illumined eyes
I gaze and dream of Paradise!

The skies have caught a tenderer light,
The great stars burn more gladly bright,
The odorous dews fall light, and steep
My soul in love-dream soft and deep ;

And every hour I live to bless
That Power whose loving tenderness
Willed that this erring life of mine
Should know such sacred love as thine.

Ah, tell me not of code or creed ;
Love, this is life indeed, indeed !
Time keeps no count, but crowds away
A hundred years in one short day !

THE BLUE BIRD.

When the welkin rings so gladly with the plough-men's voices cheery,
With the young lambs racing madly in the fallows making merry;
And the sunbeams, mirth provoking, chase the tantalizing shadows;
Then in winsome measure mocking comes across the distant meadows,
   " Twittery tweet, tweet, tweet!
   Life is sweet, so sweet!
   Twittery, tweet, tweet, tweet!
   Life is sweet. sweet, sweet!
   Life is sweet, so sweet!
  Twittery tweet; twittery tweet; twittery tweet!
  Life is fleet, life is sweet, so sweet!"

Budding boughs by flashing fountains, laughing winds that sway and
   toss them.
When the sun is on the mountains and the dew is on the blossom;
When the mist-wraiths seek the dingle, when the rosy dawn is breaking,
And the woods are all ajingle with the songs the birds are waking—
   " Twittery tweet, tweet, tweet!
   Life is sweet, so sweet!
   Twittery tweet, tweet, tweet!
   Gladly greet! Life so sweet!
   Life is sweet! Life is fleet!
  Twittery tweet, twittery tweet, twittery tweet!
  Life is sweet, sweet, sweet, so sweet!"

Happy bird! your notes are laden with a sweet soul promise bringing
Me the hope of some sweet Aiden with its joy bells ever ringing,
Where this passion-tortured spirit shall find rest from pain and
   sorrow,
And life's twilight shall inherit all the wealth of heaven's morrow!
   " Twittery tweet, tweet, tweet!
   Life is sweet, sweet, sweet!
   Twittery tweet, tweet, tweet!
   We repeat; we repeat;
   Heaven's retreat; promise sweet!
  Twittery tweet; twittery tweet; twittery tweet!
  Life is sweet, sweet, sweet, so sweet!"

DELIRIUM.

Delirium ! delirium !
The brain entranced and dead and numb,
The great nerve centers that control
The will and mind, the maniac soul,
Lashed, tortured, by a thousand wrongs,
Revels among new scenes and songs
Whose cadences are more than words
Can tell : Some straying tropic birds
Might, hovering 'round the polar zone,
Sing of wild joys unknown, unknown,
Regardless of all natural laws,
Confound the startled Esquimaux
Who hear with awe and wonder dumb—
Delirium, delirium !

Delirium, delirium !
The bitterist cynic overcome ;
The stolid stoic breaks his rule,
Takes lessons in another school,
Inhales a fair and freer breath
Along the border land of death
Than mortal lips have ever drawn ;
The soul, no longer held in pawn,
Throws off the weary chains that bind
To reason's realm the maddened mind :
And Fancy, Psyche's wanton child,
In reckless mood, insanely wild ;
One frightful plunge into the gloom,
Then thy weird light, delirium !

Delirium, delirium !
Deep the deafening thunders boom ;
Dazzling bright the lightning's play ;
Chaotic spirits wield and sway
The forces of the world, and, fraught
With power, they wrench the chains of thought

Asunder, and the visions fade
And flash anew, and dreams are made
To come and go at will, poor ghosts
Of ruined reason's vanquished hosts.
Red-handed Frenzy first enslaves,
Kills, buries, dances on their graves;
Recks not, heeds not, the frown of fate,
The smile of destiny, the prate
Of hopes that sing themselves to sleep
Among the shadows of thy doom,
Delirium! delirium!

THE ABBEY OF HOPE.

TO MRS. GALCAREN, OF HOPE NURSERY.

Dear Lady Abbess, in thy face
Calm faith and sweet content I trace;
Reflected from thy sinless heart,
The smiles that light thine eyes impart
A saintly grace and beauty rare
That God's own hand hath written there!

Here in thy cloister's sweet repose,
The new blown lily and the rose
Their richest fragance softly blend,
And odors sweet to heaven ascend
From violet, with downcast head,
And radiant fuchsia, blushing red.

" Hope "—rightly named : true Abbess thou
A benediction on thy brow;
Thy voice a blessing to console,
And in thy pure, unsullied soul,
Fair hopes like thine own roses bloom
When all the world is wrapped in gloom!

LITTLE OLD MAN OF THE MOUNTAIN.

One dark and drear and dismal day
    Among the hills I wandered,
By bare brown trees and bowlder gray,
And rifts of withered leaves that lay
Like mute reminders of the way
    That autumn wealth was squandered.

The light was fading in the West,
When, pausing on the wintry crest
Of one that towered above the rest,
    An uncouth form
Beside me uninvited stood—
One of that weird, uncanny brood,
Who, in the desert solitude,
    Through sun and storm,
Beyond the reach of mortal scan,
Forever scheme and plot and plan
The fate and destiny of man.

His back was toward me; yet, I knew
By that wan cheek of ashen hue,
And long blanched locks, where fitful blew
    Each wintry gale,
Who it was, as he stood recounting
    A doleful tale.
" 'Tis the Little Old Man of the Mountain!"

" Yes, I am he, of whom they tell,
That speak of mystic sprites that dwell
In haunted cave and gruesome glen,
Far from the traveled track of men.
    My home is nigh
Where the chime of the silvery fountain
    Echoes; and I
Am the Little Old Man of the Mountain!

Six sons, high-born and brave, each one—
Six daughters fair to look upon;
Eleven now are dead and gone,
And with the twelfth one, here alone,
   I catch each breath,
And, the heart's faint flutterings counting,
   I wait on death,"
Groaned the Little Old Man of the Mountain!

" Young January, my first born,
Was first to die; and with the morn
Came February, whose brief reign
Scarce rose ere it began to wane.
   The shrouded earth
And the night winds querulous chanting,
   Even from his birth,"
Sighed the Little Old Man of the Mountain!

" But March avenged his brother's wrongs,
And April crooned regretful songs;
And tears wrung from the saddest hours
Brought back to life the faded flowers
   That winsome May,
In her maidenly glee, kept counting
   From day to day,"
Sobbed the Little Old Man of the Mountain.

" The odorous breath of queenly June
Set all the forest choir atune
From dewy dawn to dusky eve;
And still the whispering south winds grieve
   O'er her sad fate,
And the wail in the song of the fountain
   Sounds desolate,"
Moaned the Little Old Man of the Mountain.

" Then proud and languid July came,
In whose bright eye there burned the flame
Of summer lust. And next his twin,

Imperious August, with the din
    Of tropic storms,
And the warrior's insolent vaunting,"—
    Thus waxing warm,
Cried the Little Old Man of the Mountain.

" September cooled the heated noon,
And hung the burnished harvest moon
Above his castle gate, and died.
Blue-eyed October came, the pride
    Of my old age,
In her life not a charm was wanting,"
Wailed the Little Old Man of the Mountain.

" November, born a fretful child,
Lived till the chill blast grew so wild,
She closed her troubled, tear-dimmed eyes,
And slept beneath the sullen skies!"
    His voice was low,
And was timed to the plaint of the fountain
    In deepest woe—
Poor Little Old Man of the Mountain!

" December, last of all that claim
A kinship with my fated name,
In mortal pain lies gasping now,
With death-damps gathering on her brow."
    A sudden chill
Stopped the quivering plash of the fountain,
    And cold and still
Was the Little Old Man of the Mountain.

MY LOVER IN RICHMOND.

I have a lover in Richmond,
  And her eyes, so bonny blue,
Reflect the sunshine in her soul
  And her heart so warm and true.
I have a lover in Richmond,
  Though her name I dare not tell—
So often has she told me so
  That I know she loves me well.

The flowers that bloom around Richmond,
  And the winds that sweep the sea,
And the birds that sing so blithely there—
  They all know that she loves me.
There flows a river by Richmond,
  And upon each gentle swell
A tender message thrills my heart,
  For I know she loves me well!

So fair my lady of Richmond
  That, in shame, the roses turn
Aside their heads, and those bright eyes
  Make the stars with envy burn.
To claim my lady of Richmond
  Might a monk forsake his cell—
But she is mine, and mine alone,
  And I know she loves me well!

Green be the valleys of Richmond,
  And undimm'd the summer skies;
May sunshine gild the placid seas
  Where her boat at anchor lies.
Soft blow the winds about Richmond.
  Where my fondest hopes all dwell
And all the joy I ask on earth
  Is to know she loves me well!

LITTLE ONE, SLEEP.

Little one, sleep !
Dear withered bud ! we will not weep,
  For God, in His wise providence,
  Knew best and took thy spirit hence.
And where His angels vigil keep,
    Little one, sleep !

Little one, sleep !
In restful slumber soft and deep,
  Beneath the brown November leaves,
  Where the wind of autumn moans and grieves :
Though wintry tears thy grave shall steep,
    Little one, sleep !

Little one, sleep !
For soon the April sun shall peep
  Above the hills, green leaves will spring,
  Around thy bed wild birds will sing,
And springtime's earliest roses creep—
    Little one, sleep !

Little one, sleep !
Ne'er dreaming of the storms that sweep
  The human soul when mortal sin,
  And foes without and fears within
New griefs on bitterest anguish heap—
    Little one, sleep !

Little one, sleep !
Thy happier lot shall be to reap
  Joys with no sorrows dark to sow ;
  Smiles where no blinding tears must flow ;
From life to life one painless leap—
    Little one, sleep !

Little one, sleep!
Thy memory in our hearts we keep,
Striving to turn the joy we miss
Into a hope of holier bliss,
When these dimmed eyes no more shall weep—
Little one, sleep!

LOVE ME.

I wander through the blooming woods,
Where no unhallowed thought intrudes,
And song and sunshine fall in floods ;
I hear among the budding trees
Contentment sighing in the breeze,
    And even the winds reprove me,
For crying out 'mid scenes like these,
    "Love me ! Love me ! Love me !"

I mingle with, yet walk apart,
The crowds that throng the busy mart,
And silent bear my breaking heart,
And live—Oh, life ! with pain replete,
So sweetly sad, so sadly sweet,
    With only one hope to move me;
These echoing heart-throbs still repeat,
    " Love me ! Love me ! Love me !"

The pinions of the day are furled,
And night enshrouds the sleeping world ;
But still, like restless billows hurled
Upon the shore, my spirits flies
From star to star with weary eyes
    Through the pitying skies above me,
And in its hopeless anguish cries,
    " Love me ! Love me ! Love me ! "

ISABEL, MY LADY.

Face aglow with life and hope,
　Love and light, My Lady,
The daygod climbs the dew-gemmed slope
　Beaming bright, My Lady;
Morning's brow, so lightly kissed,
Blushes through her veil of mist;
　　Isabel, My Lady!

Earth is glad when day is young;
　One by one, My Lady,
Each dumb creature finds a tongue
　In unison, My Lady.
My thrilling heart is ringing, too;
I laugh, and sing, and think of you,
　　Isabel, My Lady!

And every bloom beneath my feet,
　Looking up, My Lady,
With many a promise rare and sweet
　Fills the cup, My Lady.
Anticipation's low refrain—
"Soon shall I see thy face again,
　　Isabel, My Lady!"

With swift, impatient steps, I come
　Soon to meet My Lady,
Lips with heart-full joy grown dumb,
　I come to meet My Lady!
I gaze into those shining eyes,
Where love's light boat at anchor lies
　　Isabel, My Lady!

Awake each promised joy that sleeps
　In their beams, My Lady,
And let me have their golden deeps
　For purest dreams, My Lady;

And I will press that gentle hand
So close that you will understand,
    Isabel, My Lady!

In fond affection's tenderest tone
  I will tell, My Lady,
This tale to other ears unknown,
  " I love you well, My Lady!"
With mists and shadows cleared away
We'll live again one perfect day,
    Isabel, My Lady!

L'ENVOI.

Tho' false th' alluring fires that glow,
  All may prove, My Lady,
The faithless world can never know
  How I love My Lady!
Tho' disappointment's sombre pall
Like midnight's deepest gloom may fall;
Tho' sorrow hold my heart in thrall,
Thou art my life, my light, my all,
    Isabel, My Lady!

FAREWELL TO CEDAR VALLEY.

Farewell, farewell, a long farewell!
   Sweet City of the Valley!
Where music-murmuring waters well,
And bird-notes blithe the music swell,
   And whispering breezes dally—
And wooded height and shadowy nook,
   And all the gentle pleaders
That melt my heart with fond rebuke,
And dim my eyes as last I look
   Upon the Vale of Cedars!

When first a wanderer I came,
   Wild roses were abudding;
The maple trees were all aflame,
Burned April's cheek with maiden shame;
   A golden light was flooding
The valleys and the swelling slopes,
   The skies with promise beaming,
And all the tender trills and tropes
A-thrill with chords of cherished hopes
   And soft, sweet summer-dreaming!

'Mid purpling shades or morning dew
   My soul was ever moving
With some fresh beauty, strange and new,
And all the long, long summer through
   Kept loving, loving, loving!
I caught June's languid airs that breathed
   Rare mysteries of the mountains;
I watched the autumn mists that wreathed
Their brows till winter darts were sheathed
   Deep in the quivering fountains.

Now, when in death's pathetic hush
   December's hand hath bound thee,
I turn away to hide the rush
Of blinding tears. I cannot crush
   The ties that cling around me;

The frost is on thy pallid cheek,
  Its chill is on thy bosom ;
Wild blasts a-down the valley shriek ;
In vain with hungering heart I seek
  The purple clover blossom.

Across gray Signal's aged face
  The storm wrack's spectral shadows
Flit swiftly, and with gloom replace
The laughing gladness and the grace
  That reigned upon the meadows ;
And where the June brook hummed a song,
  Its waters ebbing, flashing,
A mountain torrent raves along,
Storm-beaten billows moan among
  The cold, black bowlders dashing !

Farewell !   But oft among my dreams
  That best-beloved elysian
Of deep green vales, and running streams,
And crested peaks, and golden gleams,
  Shall dawn upon my vision,
Where bright-eyed joy on buoyant wings
  Floats in the sun-gilt splendor
Of mists that rise from hidden springs,
Where fair Euharlee sighs and sings
  Her love-songs true and tender.

WHIP POOR WILL.

When purpling shadows westward creep,
And stars through crimson curtains peep.
And south winds sing themselves to sleep ;
From woodlands heavy with perfume
Of spicy bud and April bloom,
Comes through the tender twilight gloom,
      Music most mellow,
       " Whip po' Will—Will oh !
       Whip po' Will—Will, oh !
Whip po' Will, Whip po' Will, Whip po' Will—Will, oh!'

The bosom of the brook is filled
With new alarm, the forest thrilled
With startled echoes, and most skilled
To run a labyrinthine race,
The fireflies light their lamps to chase
The culprit through the darkling space—
      Mischievous fellow,
       " Whip po' Will—Will, oh !
       Whip po' Will—Will, oh !
Whip po' Will, Whip po' Will, Whip po' Will—Will, oh!"

From hill to hill the echoes fly,
The marshy brakes take up the cry,
And where the slumbering waters lie
In calm repose, and slyly feeds
The snipe among the whispering reeds,
The tale of this wild sprite's misdeeds
      Troubles the billow :
       " Whip po' Will—Will, oh !
       Whip po' Will—Will, oh !
Whip po' Will, Whip po' Will, Whip po' Will—Will, oh!"

And where is he of whom they speak ?
Is he just playing hide and seek
Among the thickets up the creek ?
Or is he resting from his play

In some cool grotto, far away,
Where lullaby-crooning zephyrs stray,
   Smoothing his pillow,
    " Whip po' Will—Will, oh !
    Whip po' Will—Will, oh !
Whip po' Will, Whip po' Will, Whip po' Will—Will, oh!"

BEYOND THE STARS.

There is a land beyond the stars
   Where I shall rest some day,
Healing the scars of the wasting wars
   That are wearing my life away;
Drying the eye that wearily weeps,
   Soothing the agony sore ;
Contentment sleeps in those azure deeps,
   And my heart shall ache no more !

There hope in sweet and sure release
   Each dream shall realize,
And every breeze that sweeps the seas
   Echoes its satisfied sighs ;
Grown pure and strong from paths of wrong,
   My spirit shall gladly soar,
And I'll turn my sorrow into a song
   And my heart shall ache no more !

Forgotten the fears and the blinding tears
   That shadow this sin-cursed sod,
Illumed by a glorious light that cheers
   From the face of the living God;
No longer ahead glooms the haunting dread
   The future may hold in store ;
Rapt with the beauties around me spread,
   And my heart shall ache no more !

Though the night of death fall chill and cold,
   And the way be dark and drear,
Dawn shall unfold with a joy untold
   As I wake in its brightness there.
Fairer than Fancy's imaging fine,
   Or Philosophy's deepest lore,
Is the life divine that will all be mine,
   And my heart shall ache no more !

Beyond the stars I shall seek and find
   Fulfillment of each desire
That has thrilled my mind, in its groping blind,
   With a wild, unearthly fire:
Blooming and bright with a new delight,
   I shall walk on a sun-blessed shore,
No longer to roam like a child of the night,
   And my heart shall ache no more!

THE COMING OF WINTER.

There's a cloud on the brow of the mountain,
   A mistiness hangs on the vale;
A film dulls the flash of the fountain,
   There's a sob in the sigh of the gale.
All the brightness the summer king brought them
   Is dimmed by the sadness of Autumn,
   The pensive forebodings of Autumn!

The golden rod bloometh in splendor,
   The sumach's red banners float free;
And the rich purple meadow weeds render
   The woodlands most wondrous to see,
With the glories the season hath wrought them
   Rich dyes for the mantle of Autumn,
   The glamour and glory of Autumn!

A wail that is piteously thrilling,
  And sad as a lover's last words,
Is heard in the tremulous, trilling
  Farewells of the lingering birds !
Sad lays that the chill winds have taught them
  To chant at the coming of Autumn,
  The plaint and the pathos of Autumn !

The harvest fields, shriveled and sober,
  The unfruitful fallows all brown,
Have yielded to solemn October
  Their jewels to weave in her crown.
With the grasp of a miser she caught them
  To weave in the diadem of Autumn ;
  The costly crown-jewels of Autumn !

In the distant abyss of dark heaven,
  From the pitiless, glittering eyes
Of the stars, cheerless glances are given
  Earthward from the cold, dreary skies.
Not the guardian spirits we thought them,
  But the slavish magicians of Autumn,
  Of the magic and mystery of Autumn !

And faded the hopes that I cherished
  Since Summer's full pulse-beats are stilled—
With the dream of the Summer they perished—
  And their promises all unfulfilled !
Ah, vainly in sorrow I sought them
  'Mid the wreck and the ruin of Autumn,
  The dark desolation of Autumn !

Oh God ! How I clung to my treasures,
  With devotion deep, passionate, wild,
From a heart that is willful, and measures
  Its desires like an unreasoning child ;
But I know now how dearly I bought them ;
  Like the life-purchased pleasures of Autumn,
  The death-doomed enjoyments of Autumn !

THEY WILL MISS YOU.

I am sure the birds will miss you
      Bye and bye;
Whispering winds will long to kiss you
      When the sky
Wears a veil of teary sadness,
Shadowing the summer gladness,
      When you die!

Flashing waters, lowly humming
      Out of tune,
Blossoms bright, that loved your coming
      As a boon;
Smile no more, but grieve and wonder—
Busy bees will sadly ponder
      As they croon!

Starry eyes of night will glisten
      Through their tears;
Chant the whip-poor-will and listen
      Through the years,
Ever sighing and recalling
That 'tis not your light step falling
      That he hears!

Children, too, with sober faces,
      They will tell
How that you, with all your graces,
      Loved them well!
Treasured memories will awaken
With your name, in hearts forsaken,
      Isabel!

But one heart e'en now must languish,
      Sob and moan—

Bear its load of pain and anguish—
    And unknown,
Like some tortured soul unshriven,
Watch the guarded gates of heaven,
    All alone !

Yes, I know the world will miss you
    When life's done ;
But I envy now the winds that kiss you,
    And the sun
Who, with rapturous caresses,
Touches now your shining tresses—
    Happy one !

From December to December,
    All the way
Through life's decline will I remember
    That bright day
When, upon your snowy bosom,
Bloomed a spray of apple blossom
    In the May !

Oh ! the words I cannot fashion,
    Though I try ;
For th' unfathomed depth of passion
    Drowns the cry !
You will know it all and feel it,
When mists of earth no more conceal it—
    Bye and bye !

MY LADY'S EYES.

My Lady's eyes
Are like the dyes
Of Indian summer's bluest skies ;
And in their deeps
An angel keeps
His watch, while infant Cupid sleeps.

Her brow is white
As snow, and bright
As April's incandescent light,
When south-winds bring
And gently fling
Their treasures at the feet of Spring.

Nor dark nor fair
Her twining hair,
But all the rays of evening share ;
Each tender touch
And tint is such,
I only know I love them much.

The rich rays seek
Her rounded cheek,
Like sunbeams clustering 'round some peak
Where ebbs and flows
And burns and glows
The blended light of suns and snows.

Her sweet breath tips
Those rosy lips
With honey dew the brown bee sips
From fragrant flowers,
In woodland bowers,
At evening's calm and tranquil hours.

Ah, Lady mine,
May light divine
From fairest suns around thee shine,
Till golden skies
Before thee rise
Beyond the walls of Paradise!

HER EYES.

O wondrous eyes!
Within their depths the blended dyes
  Of every star that brightest glows,
  Of tenderest tints that paint the rose,
Of purest rays of sunset skies—
    O wondrous eyes!

Expressive eyes!
Hiding the thought that in them lies,
  Yet, in their efforts to conceal
  Another secret they reveal,
Of some new joy, some sweet surprise—
    Expressive eyes!

O glorious eyes!
Full of the genial warmth that dries
  The last drop from the bitterest cup,
  And bids the suffering soul look up
Toward hope's inviting paradise—
    O glorious eyes!

Ah, tender eyes!
That softly shine through sobs and sighs,
  That mourn the sad and cruel fate
  Of love that came, but came too late,
And o'er this cruel sacrifice
    Weep, tender eyes!

LONELINESS.

I am lonely, oh, so lonely !
And I think if I could only
    See her face,
I could warm my heart and sun it
In the light that shines upon it,
    And the grace
In her eyes like beams from heaven,
When some sinner stands forgiven
    In its ray;
And the shackles fall asunder
'Mid that new life's golden wonder,
    Far away !

In my memory still lingers
The soft touch of fairy fingers,
    But I miss
That sweet comfort of her presence—
That divine, delicious pleasance,
    Purest bliss
That can thrill a mortal bosom,
Add a tint to every blossom
    On the spray;
And the tones the angels taught her
Mock the rythm of falling water
    Far away !

There's a melancholy madness
In the sunshine, and a sadness
    And a swoon;
All the stars have lost their lustre,
And the dismal cloud wracks cluster
    'Round the moon !
And the songful winds are listless
Since my soul has lost its mistress;
    And the day

And its brightness are bereft me—
Now that she has gone and left me,
    Far away!

Birds are lisping, bees are humming,
With the gladness of her coming,
    And I know
That there's not an accent wanting
In the winsome waters' chanting
    As they flow:
Chills my soul with bleak December
When her absence I remember,
    Though 'tis May;
When the odorous airs are ringing
With the songs that she is singing
    Far away!

Oh, impatient thoughts are thronging
Almost hopeless, yet still longing
    As I yearn,
Through the days that drag so dreary,
Through the nights that hang so weary,
    Her return!
Ere I close my eyes in slumber,
Every lonely hour I number,
    While I pray
That God's angels bright may render
Every blessing and attend her
    Far away!

I LOVE SOMEBODY.

At the foot of the mountain a silvery brook
  Goes merrily, cheerily, tripping along,
By lichen-grey boulder and shadowy nook,
  Rehearsing its rythmical burden of song,
In strains of deep passion that tenderly flow :
  " I love somebody, I love somebody ;
I love somebody, I know—I know—
    I love somebody, I know ! "

On the uppermost twig of a light swaying bough,
  A wild bird is dreamily trilling his lay ;
The murmured refrain of a true lover's vow,
  That lightens the hours of a long summer day,
With rapturous melody, soft, sweet and low :
  " I love somebody, I love somebody,
I love somebody, I know—I know—
    I love somebody, I know ! "

And the whispering west wind its love-laden sighs
  Deliciously breathes in my hungering soul,
Perfumed with the fragrant aromas that rise
  From flowery thicket and bloom-scented knoll,
And pools where the pond lily's starry eyes glow :
  " I love somebody, I love somebody,
I love somebody, I know—I know—
    I love somebody, I know ! "

Flow on, flashing waters ; your musical trills
  In unison tuned with my heart's fondest note ;
Sing on happy lover, the carol that thrills
  My soul as it swells from thy quivering throat !
Westwind, in bewildering ecstacy blow—
  For I love somebody, I love somebody,
I love somebody, I know—I know—
    I love somebody I know !

I'LL NEVER COME BACK TO YOU.

Ah, heart of my heart! The moon may rise
  In splendor most divine ;
In fathomless depths of purpling skies
  The stars in splendor shine ;
The carol of birds in woodlands deep
  Where sunbeams sip the dew ;
The wanderer's eye will wake to weep.
    For I'll never come back to you, love—
      I'll never come back to you !

Ah, love of my love! When gladsome Spring
  Comes dancing down the glen ;
When whip-poor-wills make the echoes ring
  In darkling depths again ;
When storm-beaten branch and leafless bough
  In freshness bloom anew,
The breeze will fan one aching brow,
    For I'll never come back to you, love—
      I'll never come back to you !

Oh, soul of my soul! When riotous brooks
  Through ranks of waving fern
Are brawling their songs in shadowy nooks,
  In joy o'er summer's return ;
When quivering field and shimmering sky
  Assume their mellowest hue,
Then out of the depths my soul shall cry,
    For I'll never come back to you, love—
      I'll never come back to you !

Ah, life of my life! A hungering pain
  Will weigh my spirit down,
When mournfully hangs a fringe of rain

On woodlands autumn brown.
From season to season those days of bliss
  And joys that once I knew
Shall haunt my spirit, and saddest is this,
  That I'll never come back to you, love—
    I'll never come back to you!

A WOMAN'S WORD.

I told you nay when last we met;
I know 'tis inconsistent, yet,
Upon reflection, I confess
Wells from my heart the answer " Yes!"
Uncertain as a humming-bird
Upon the wing, a woman's word!

    *   *   *

I love you, but I've changed my mind;
I do not mean to be unkind;
I see it in a different light,   .
And really must say " No," to-night.
No leaf by varying breezes stirred
So changeful as a woman's word.

    *   *   *

Oh, love, pray press your lips to mine,
Once more your arms around me twine;
Now, that life's tide is ebbing fast,
I will be consistent, true, at last!
Heartsick from hope too long deferred—
A woman's word! A woman's word!

"O! CHAMOUNI."

Without the night was dark and chill,
All sounds were hushed, the winds were still;
The glowing stars shone bright and fair
Thro' depths of crisp November air.
Then came to my delighted ear
A sweet voice, rising soft and clear;
That voice of matchless harmony
Sang " Chamouni, sweet Chamouni ! "

I paused a shadowy tree beneath,
Entranced I stood and held my breath.
That sweet and low half-pensive swell,
Which on the night air rose and fell,
Was like the tender, wooing sighs
That soft winds breathe 'neath southern skies.
Such pure, delicious harmony—
" O! Chamouni, sweet Chamouni ! "

I knew that vale was far away
Where Alpine winter, wan and gray,
'Neath skies where burns the hectic glow,
Sits throned amid wild wastes of snow.
And this young heart was throbbing now
With rich, warm, southern blood, and how
And whence this burst of harmony—
" O! Chamouni, sweet Chamouni ! "

The cheerful light assistance lent ;
With stealthy steps my course I bent,
And noiselessly I entered where
There sat a maiden young and fair.
So light she touched the trembling keys
Methought she feared she might displease
The sprite that lent this harmony—
" O! Chamouni, sweet Chamouni ! "

The drooping lashes half concealed
The kindling love-light, half revealed
Within those soft, brown eyes that shone
Like twilight in some tropic zone,
And softened by some fairy spell
Like sacred chime of silver bell,
Her voice a perfect harmony—
" O! Chamouni, sweet Chamouni ! "

And never more can I forget
That air which haunts my mem'ry yet.
Sweet echoes from some far-off shore—
Rare, touching strains ne'er heard before ;
Thrills half of pleasure, half of pain,
Sweet voice I ne'er shall hear again,
Enchanting, rapturous harmony,
"O! Chamouni, sweet Chamouni !"

OCTOBER.

TO A FRIEND ON HER BIRTHDAY.

Once more our princess hath unrolled
  Her silken tresses brown,
Burnished with misty dust of gold,
  From Summer's broken crown.

And blue-eyed Autumn's favorite child,
  Enthroned upon the hills,
With wondrous beauty, rich and wild,
  The merry woodland fills.

She comes to add another pearl
  Unto that silver thread ;
Another year scarce weighs a curl
  Upon that queenly head !

May thrice as many more, my love,
    Be added ; then I ween
October, princess now, will prove
    Well worthy to be queen.

And may your own sweet, starry eyes
    With undimmed lustre shine,
As now, with love's first shy surprise,
    They look straight into mine!

IT IS SO SAD TO DIE!

TO THE MEMORY OF WALES WYNTON.

When May is blooming into June,
    And Summer days are nigh ;
When pleasure sings her sweetest tune,
When glory points to mounting noon,
    It is so sad to die!

The sun sinks down the western skies,
    The stars shine forth on high ;
As fade the sunset's changing dyes,
The lifelight faded from his eyes ;
    It is so sad to die!

And he so bright, so brave, so young!
    A sparkling spring gone dry ;
A blighted branch where green leaves hung,
A sweet-toned harp that's all unstrung—
    It is so sad to die!

Come closer, mother, bend thine ear,
    And catch the faint, low sigh ;
It is the last that thou shalt hear
Forever more from lips so dear—
    It is so sad to die!

'Tis passed! Where conflicts were so rife
    No shadows 'round him lie ;
To earth the sorrow, pain, and strife,
The sadness all belongs to life—
    It is not sad to die!

THAT LITTLE BLACK CREPE BONNET.

Had I the poet's pleasing power
  I'd pen a dainty sonnet,
Not to some fair and transient flower
That blooms within my lady's bower,
But I would raptured measures shower
  On that little black crepe bonnet!

No jeweled diadem ever claimed
  A queenlier head to don it,
Nor scheming Nature ever aimed
That brighter radiance had shamed
The sunshine, than the face that's framed
  In that little black crepe bonnet!

A puzzling question 'tis, to me,
  A pleasure, too, to con it;
I know I never can be free,
Nor ever can quite happy be,
Until I solve the mystery
  Of that little black crepe bonnet!

There's not an extra turn or touch
  That I can see upon it,
Yet there's an air about it such
That I, bewildered, vainly clutch
At every clue—I'm worried much
  By that little black crepe bonnet!

There's not a feather, fringe or frill
  Or a bit of ribbon on it
Unusual; still for good or ill
There's magic that might cure or kill,
And I, poor foolish dreamer, will
  Love that little black crepe bonnet!

The happiest man on earth were I
   To know that I had won it,
With its fair wearer, proud and shy
In all her radiant beauty—why,
Look! There she goes a-tripping by
   With that little black crepe bonnet!

A TRIBUTE.

TO THE MEMORY OF JAMES H. CAMPBELL, PROPRIETOR OF THE MACON TELEGRAPH.

Hope in the morning soared on high,
   With plumage white as snow new driven,
But fluttered, feebly, home to die,
   On torn and ble-ding wings at even'.
With deepest grief my heart is wrung
That hope so bright should die so young.

And o'er my soul a storm has swept—
   Its bitterest drops still dim my eyes,
Such as heart-broken Adam wept
   When gazing last on Paradise,
As night, thrice darkened by the frown
Of an offended God, came down.

How cold and cruel art thou, Death!
   To rend such loving friends apart;
To steal away that precious breath,
   And chill for aye that generous heart!
Why cut him down before his time,
Just in manhood's glorious prime?

Why force the draught from that dark stream,
   Whose waters, deep and cold, possess
The power to quench Life's fondest dream
   In deep and long forgetfulness?
Was there naught else that we might give,
And let our choicest spirit live?

But he is gone!   His weary feet
  Shall press time's desert sands no more.
I can but pray that we may meet
  One day upon some fairer shore;
Beyond this land of grief and pain
Such soul as his must live again.

Although in gloom I sit and sigh,
  I feel that he is happier now;
Though closed to earth that sparkling eye,
  And still and cold that pallid brow—
His soul was tired, and God knew best,
And kindly took him home to rest.

TUBE-ROSES.

TO ONE WHO WORE THEM IN HER HAIR.

Tube-roses!
Rare and passing fair
  As maiden's brightest dream,
Their breath perfumes the evening air
While in my lady's shining hair
  The star-eyed blossoms gleam.

Tube-roses—
Fragrant, fresh and sweet,
  They are to me a part
Of such dear memories, fond though fleet,
As quicken every throb and beat
  That thrills my inmost heart.

Tube-roses!
Modest, pure and chaste,
  'Neath blue September skies,
Into life's dull and cheerless waste
Their gentle presence brings a taste
  Of man's lost paradise!

5

THE LAST DAY OF SUMMER.

'Tis the last day of summer, My Lady,
  And sunset is gilding the west,
As I sit here and watch for your coming,
  My Lady, that loves me the best!

My eyes they are weary with watching,
  And over the landscape so fair
A shadowy mantle is falling,
  The gloom of a hopeless despair!

Rare summer! The fairest and fleetest
  That brought you and made you my own!
Rare summer! The saddest and sweetest
  That ever this wild heart has known!

'Tis the last day of summer, My Lady,
  My waiting and watching are vain;
As I sit here and long for your coming
  And know that you'll come not again!

I sit here and sigh for your coming,
  O! come in your beauty and grace,
And let me stay here in the twilight
  And gaze on your radiant face.

No planet that burns in the heavens,
  'Mid clearest of October skies,
Compares with the light that is beaming
  In the depths of your luminous eyes.

No music of soft-falling water,
  Nor bird-note in summer-green grove,
So sweet to my soul and so soothing
  As the sound of that voice that I love.

But the brightness and glory have faded,
  And hushed is the soul-cheering voice,
Tho' the skies shine again in new splendor
  And the woods with new music rejoice.

For me 'tis the last day of summer,
  And sad-hearted autumn has come
To bury the hopes that I cherished,
  And weep by their desolate tomb !

THE DEATH OF SUMMER.

Low in the west the hectic flush,
  The doom of day implying :
Across the skies the storm wracks rush,
And swiftly fades the last faint blush—
  Dying, dying, dying !

Around King Summer's couch of pain
  September gales are sighing,
While sadly falls the mournful rain,
Like one who weeps and weeps in vain—
  Dying, dying, dying !

And weird and wild there comes a wail—
  A night bird shrilly crying—
And shivering in her widow's veil
The rayless moon sits wan and pale—
  Dying, dying, dying !

The shuddering maples cast their leaves
  Grim death takes no denying ;
Though Nature's troubled spirit grieves
While gathering in her harvest sheaves —
  Dying, dying, dying !

No more through purpling shadows come
  The blithesome echoes flying;
Drear autumn taps the muffled drum
Through desolate woodlands dark and dumb—
  Dying, dying, dying!

Out of the silent night I call
  To one whose form is lying
Beneath the withering turf, and all
The sound that pierces night's dark pall—
  " Dying, dying, dying! "

UNFURL YOUR BANNER.

Unfurl your banner, Christians!
  To the pure soft breeze of heaven,
Let none remain of all that train
  Of sinners unforgiven.

Unfurl your banner, Christians!
  Beneath its folds divine
In reverence heard that magic word—
  " Jesus! " the countersign.

Unfurl your banner, Christians!
  Shake out its purple hem;
Along your lines in splendor shines
  The Star of Bethlehem.

Unfurl your banner, Christians!
  Lift up your standard high!
Let the broad girth of heaven and earth
  Echo your battle cry.

Unfurl your banner, Christians!
  And march to victory,
For it shall wave beyond the grave
  In Heaven's eternity.

WHEN SHALL I SEE THE SUN?

Oh, clouds that drift in sorrow
  Across the leaden sky,
Pray tell me if, to-morrow,
  The sun shall shine on high.
Or is it thus they perished,
  The joys so dearly won,
The dream so fondly cherished—
  When shall I see the sun?

My heart is sunk in sadness,
  None guess the bitter woe
That goads my soul to madness.
  No matter where I go.
No bird of hope is singing
  Its song of tasks well done,
But requiem bells are ringing—
  When shall I see the sun?

The stars may set in splendor,
  In splendor rise again ;
New flowers may bloom as tender
  Beneath the summer rain.
But man, Misfortune's plaything,
  Once down, Life's favors shun :
Long he may watch the dayspring.
  And never see the sun!

I've lost the flowers I gathered
  In valleys green and gay;
Unwatered, dry and withered,
  They mark my lonely way;
No stone, though I'm so weary,
  To lay my head upon :
Though night falls dark and dreary—
  When shall I see the sun?

THE DREAM OF AARON BURR.

As I con the page of history and step by step retrace
The unfolding of the mystery, the peopling of the space,
Of those undiscovered regions that beyond the river lay
Where he marshalled all the legions that his fancy held in sway ;
With the valleys and the mountains and the stretch of fertile plains,
Lakes and streams and living fountains yielding up their golden gains ;
Oft the wonder of the story and its amplitude recur,
Through the glamour and the glory of the dream of Aaron Burr !

From the broad and blue Pacific to the Gulf of Mexico,
From those tropic lands prolific to perpetual peaks of snow ;
With the waste of wild Sierras and the plains of Arkansaw,
With the mines of Cordilleras and the ports of Panama ;
Swept his vision on the pinions of ambition grown so bold,
That the scope of his dominions half a continent controlled ;
Reckless, daring and undaunted, whom no danger could deter,
The gorgeous empire-haunted dream of dashing Aaron Burr !

He would set his throne in splendor, proud Napoleon of the West,
Every charm that power can render would his royalty invest ;
Mighty hosts would march victorious with his banner floating free,
Ships of battle, grand and glorious, would in triumph sweep the sea ;
From exalted domes of learning brands of wisdom would be hurled,
And each torch of knowledge burning would illumine all the world ;
While the stride of man's advancement set the universe astir,
With his own great name's enhancement in the dream of Aaron Burr !

Fearless, fascinating, kingly ! born to lead his fellow-men,
Braved a mighty nation singly ; beaten, but not conquered, then
Watched the hand of Fate undoing every project that he loved,
And beheld the wreck and ruin of his fortunes, all unmoved ;
Bravely chose alone to wander forth upon a foreign shore,
Rather than his plea should pander to the pride of men who wore
Power's cheap tinselled badge of Faction he would banishment prefer,
Crowning conquest, life and action, filled the dream of Aaron Burr !

From the storm of Revolution and the camp of Washington,
From chaos to Constitution, many a deed of daring done :
Then with equal valor wielded in the council of the state
Weapons of the mind, and yielded to no foeman in debate ;
With the mark of Cain deep branded on his forehead, doomed to roam
Up and down the earth red-handed, far from country friends and home.
Blennerhasset—dark dishonor—Theodosia ! Through the blur
Of the fate that fell upon her, fades the dream of Aaron Burr !

TO THE MEMORY OF A HAPPY DAY.

When fell the light of morning
    On field and wood and stream,
The dull gray rocks adorning
    With many a silvery beam :
When trembled on each leafy spray
    A diadem bright of dew,
Up the wooded heights I took my way
    And oft I thought of you.

I reached the misty summit
    When the noontide reigned on high,
And the light clouds floated slowly
    Across the soft May sky ;
And I turned my face toward the east,
    Toward the dim horizon blue
And I thought of a day that now is past,
    And then I thought of you.

I stood on Signal Mountain
    And watched the sun go down,
In robes of royal splendor
    Behind the mountains brown ;
Their last rays touched each purple peak
    With a gorgeous, golden hue ;
With a heart too full of love to speak,
    I gazed—and thought of you.

REMORSE.

Wayward, willful, prone to wander
　　From the paths of truth and right,
Every Godlike gift to squander
　　In the wastes of vain delight!
As I watch the storm-clouds gather,
　　Wreck and ruin in their train,
I would give this world, O Father!
　　Just to be myself again!

Dimmed the hopes that shone sublimely,
　　Summer-dreams that faded fast;
Down the vale of life untimely
　　Sweeps the Autumn's withering blast!
Doubts and fears are gathering 'round me,
　　Shadowing all I longed to be!
Severing all the ties that bound me,
　　In my weakness, Lord, to Thee!

Madly gnaws the wild heart-hunger,
　　And the cold and cruel clasp
Of this dark remorse grows stronger—
　　Faints my soul within its clasp!
Ghosts of Memory's weird creation
　　Menace now, with threatening frown,
In the gloom and desolation,
　　Where the star of Faith went down!

In my weak and helpless fashion,
　　From the depths of black despair,
In Thine own divine compassion,
　　Father, hear my penitent prayer!
With my sins and sorrows take me,
　　This the burden of my plea:
Cleanse my heart, O God! and make me
　　All that Thou wouldst have me be!

ONE HOUR WITH THEE.

One hour with thee, when in the dell
The twilight's tawny shadows fell,
Checkered with bars of silvery sheen
That fell from purpling skies serene,
Where, in the sunset's fading light,
Queen regnant of the summer night,
In splendor shone the maiden moon :
And crickets chirped a pleasant tune,
And katydids low vespers hummed,
And in the darkling branches drummed
The drone of some belated bee ;
I spent the last sweet hour with thee.

One hour with thee ! So silent then,
With thoughts too deep for mortal ken;
Involved in that delicious trance,
Our hearts too full for utterance,
Our spirits blended into one,
Our pulse-beats timed in unison;
We watched the day's departing glow
And caught the cadence sweet and low,
Of summer winds that swept the woods,
Filling the scented solitudes
With strains of music wild and free--
One hour with thee, one hour with thee !

One hour with thee ! Can I forget,
Though by the cares of life beset,
The warm hand-clasp, the soft caress,
The look of melting tenderness;
The greeting smile, the parting sigh,
And then, at last, the fond " good-bye ! "
And after we such joys have known,
In sadness each must walk alone,
And hide beneath each placid brow
A heavy heart that's aching now ;
Oh ! how I long, and long, to be
If but an hour—one hour—with thee !

MY WIFE'S PICTURE.

Ever before me that dear face,
  So calm and patient, pure and true;
In every curve and line I trace
Divinest beauty, rarest grace,
  Human perfection ever knew.

In those brave eyes, the radiant light
  Of trusting faith and love, deep drawn.
Still burns unclouded, clear and bright
As when my eyes first read aright
  The illumined skies of love's fair dawn.

Above that shining brow there gleams
  A coronet of shining hair,
Gilt with the light one sees in dreams;
So rich the varying tints it seems
  Imprisoned sunbeams languish there!

Upon that rounded cheek the sheen
  Of summer mornings concentrate;
'Twixt those half-parted lips serene,
A lurking smile of joy, I ween,
  But mocks the darkest frown of Fate.

But oh! this cunning counterfeit
  Scarce half portrays my lady's grace,
Leaving the brilliancy and wit
With which that high-born soul is lit.
  And painter's hand can never trace!

Here at her feet my soul I fling;
  Whate'er of joy or grief betide,
I ask of life but this one thing:
That she accept my offering,
  And keep me ever by her side!

REVELATION.

I knew not how fair was the blossom
    That blooms on a bare, leafless tree,
'Till close to your pure, loving bosom
    You folded a wand'rer like me!

Every clime has its own choicest season,
    But spring is the same everywhere;
Every soul has its governing reason,
    But love to all hearts is most dear.

Since the night when I first learned the story
    You taught me of light, life and love,
All the stars have grown brighter in glory
    And grandeur and beauty above.

The songs of the brooks are more tender,
    And softer the summer winds' sigh;
The sun in superior splendor
    Illumines the fair summer sky.

And sweeter the blush of the morning,
    And richer the mockingbird's note,
And purer the dew-gems adorning
    The pond-lily's delicate throat.

The fields with green harvest hopes fairer,
    More soothing the hum of the bees;
And the light and the shadows fall rarer
    Through the boughs of the low-sighing trees.

Oh! words that my lips cannot fashion—
    Lips with unmeasured ecstacy dumb:
Borne down by wild torrents of passion,
    Soul, body and mind overcome.

Dead all other emotions that move me,
    Banished nightmares of sorrow and strife;
Oh, tell me once more that you love me—
    It is all that I ask for in life.

I LOVE YOU.

"I love you!"
This sweet, simple phrase
    The purest gem of earth contains.
Not all the great world's meed of praise
Such perfect happiness conveys
Or lingers long in after days,
    When little else of joy remains.

"I love you!"
All sufficient this
    To bind the heart in chains of gold :
Like young affection's first warm kiss,
The soul desires no higher bliss,
The book of life—no leaf amiss—
    And not a sentence left untold.

"I love you!"
Swift have sped the years
    Since, like the south-wind, breathing low,
That soft voice on my raptured ears
Fell like the gentle sighs one hears
When dew-drops fall like happy tears
    Beneath the sunset's dying glow.

"I love you!"
Oh, the blessed thought
    That one true heart is all my own;
And nearer earth to heaven is brought,
While in the soul what wonders wrought !
A thousand glories new are taught,
    And hopes unfold before unknown.

"I love you!"
As the sunbeams burst
    Through clouds that shroud the sullen skies:
A star when storms are raging worst—

Soft rain to burning lips that thirst—
So comes this holiest bliss uncursed,
 A sacred joy that never dies.

  " I love you!"
All that grieves and harms
 Is driven from out the throbbing heart.
Abides a soothing peace that charms
All cares and sorrows' wild alarms,
And in those close entwining arms
 Content is found, and perfect rest.

SEPARATION.

So near and yet so far apart,
  Dear faithful heart!
Day after day we meet and greet,
  Upon the street,
With words so calm and dignified,
  Such well-feigned pride.
None guess we love—ah, none can know!—
  Each other so!

And yet, though circumspect and wise,
  Our tell-tale eyes
Give—unvoiced thoughts we dare not say—
  Our souls away;
And, wakened by their ardent beams
  From blissful dreams,
The youthful god, with mischief rife,
  Renews the strife.

So far apart, and yet so near,
  We linger here;
The radiance in your love-lit eyes
  The tear-drop dries
In mine, just as the distant sun
  Drives, one by one,
The dew-drops off, that tremble on
  The cheek of Dawn.

THE LAST FAREWELL.

Farewell !
    Ambition bore my spirit up
'Till touched my feet this dreary waste ;
    Tongue cannot tell
        How hard it is to drink this cup—
Bitterest of all that man should taste.

    Oh, God !
        The anguish of my throbbing heart
That aches and still must ache in vain—
    Cold as the clod
        That of some bleak spot forms a part,
Where falls no more the summer rain.

    I loved—
        Ah, Heaven ! How madly, wildly sweet
Those rarest of all unearthly dreams !
    Alas ! they proved
        False fires that led my wand'ring feet
By loneliest sorrow-haunted streams.

    Oh, Death !
        Mayst not thy kind though chilly hand,
In mercy, now, take this, mine own—
    E'en let my breath
        Be hushed ; lead me to that dark land
Where hope and memory are unknown.

    To-night
        I can but sit and grieve and moan
In this, my soul's dumb agony.
    From human sight
        Concealed, God only hears each groan
Of more than mortal misery !

    Good-bye !
        The only comfort left me now :
The thought, though sorrowful it be,
    That bye and bye,
        In memory of our sweet past, thou
Wilt drop one pitying tear for me !

1888–1889.

The hand, along time's dial plate,
Moves slowly, as I contemplate
Its last faint flutterings, and mark
How calmly dies the year; but hark!
The clock is striking. With a sob
The Old Year dies, and now the throb
And thrill of vigorous life strikes through
The pulsing arteries of the new.
One dies that the other may be born;
Night buries the Old that shining morn
May wed the New. Ah, the last stroke fell,
'Tis twelve o'clock, and—all is well!

FORGIVE AND FORGET.

As, when a stormy day is done,
There flashes from the dying sun
A parting smile of tender love
Ere falls the night, oh, wilt thou prove
Thyself as kind, and backward fling
One look in pity offering,
Just now when all life's ill beset me,
Forgiving if you must forget me!

My heart is heavy, and my soul
Aches with muffled bells that toll
My last hope's dreary requiem;
As, o'er the plains of Bethlehem,
The bright star of forgiveness rose,
So let the kindly light that glows
As brightly as when first you met me,—
Let those dear eyes forgive—forget me.

LIEUTENANT BARNEY LEE.

[In 1861 Captain Purtell was the only man in the Fulton Blues who had attained his majority, and the next oldest was Barney Lee, aged 19, who was commissioned First Lieutenant in the emergency. He has kept the old commission on his person every day since he received it.]

Scant five feet four, a boyish form,
A sapling youth to face the storm
Of war, that in its withering wrath
Laid strong-limbed oaks along its path.
But nineteen summers, mild and meek.
Had blown the roses on his cheek ;
Their fairy fingers wrought the casque
Of soft brown locks—a dainty task—
That bound his forehead fair and free,
The boy lieutenant, Barney Lee !

That boyish band in garb of gray,
" The Fulton Blues," drilled every day.
The call was urgent ; Governor Brown
And all his counsellors sat down
Discussing various means and ways
By which they might battalions raise.
" The Blues? We know their captain well,
A manly soldier, brave Purtell,
But should his fall stern fate decree
There's but that stripling, Barney Lee !"

" How old ?" asked Governor Brown. " Nineteen,"
Replied another. " His canteen
Will weight him down ; as for his sword
I do believe, upon my word,
That as he marches with the band
He'll trail its scabbard in the sand !"
The governor stroked his long, gray beard,
Observing slowly: " I have heard
That boys make men, sometimes, and we
Will just commission Barney Lee !"

Among the bleak Virginian hills,
Whose snows were streaked with crimson rills,
The weary march, the battle's press
Manassas and the Wilderness;
Through seven States he saw recoil
The shattered ranks who drenched the soil
With blood, from Mississippian plain
To Carolinian woods—again
Among the hills of Tennessee;
The young lieutenant, Barney Lee!

Beneath the blue Floridian sky
Olustee heard their battle cry;
With arms and ammunition gone
They hurled great ponderous blocks of stone
Upon the struggling, surging mass
Hemmed in the rugged mountain pass
Beneath old Lookout's lofty brow,
And taught the advancing foeman how
Each triumph dearly bought must be
With foes like those with Barney Lee!

With half-clad limbs and shoeless feet,.
Driven inch by inch, that long retreat,
That with a trooper marked each rod
Of federal march on Georgian sod;
The nights so drear, the days so raw.
From Cumberland hills to Kennesaw :
And wasted farm and burning town
Behind the army marching down
As Sherman's legions sought the sea—
Still in the vanguard, Barney Lee!

The fire in that dark eye grew dim
When Dixie's stirring battle hymn
Was hushed for aye! the world grew cold;
Neglected, prematurely old
His warworn brow!   Yet, mark the flash
Of light beneath his gray mustache
As he unfolds, all stained and torn,
That old commission he has borne
Nigh thirty years of grief and glee
That made " Lieutenant Barney Lee ! "

A LATE WILD ROSE.

April was bright with its tenderest light,
    And May with its wealth of flowers,
When falling in floods through the tuneful woods
    Came sunshine in silvery showers.
Fragrant was June from morn to noon,
    With aromas of woodsy musk;
And the sweet dews fell on the languid swell
    Of the wind in the golden dusk.

I loved them all from the sunflower tall
    To the diletant larkspur blue;
And no one the best for all were possessed
    Of a witchery fair and true;
But late in the year, when the leaves were sere
    And summer was growing gray,
I found a rose at the dreamful close
    Of a sweet September day.

But a late wild rose, yet strangely I chose
    To gather it close to my breast,
For because of the fate that it bloomed so late
    It was dearer than all the rest.
There is never a rose in the garden grows
    Can match its rare perfume;
There is never a hint of its delicate tint
    In a forest of bud and bloom.

Ah, I love that rose, and it feels and knows
    That my heart is most sincere,
And strong and deep, tho' I watch and weep
    In my passionate longing here
For the sorrowful fate that it bloomed too late—
    Oh, desolate grief so vain!
December snows will wither my rose,
    Found but to be lost again.

JEFF HANCOCK'S BULL.

Jeff Hancock's my neighbor. One mornin' last spring,
When skeeters were jist a beginnin' to sing,
I went over thar to git one of his plows,
And found him a pennin' a fine bunch of cows.

"What news?" says I, "neighbor, you've jist come from town?"
"No news, 'cept I've my arrangements with Brown,
To git my supplies of guanner an' bacon;
He said 'twer the fortieth mortgage he'd taken."

"You've got some fine stock." "Yes, jist look at that calf;
He's the fines' bull yearlin' round 'ere by half;
His horns sets jist right, and do look what a neck!
His daddy's half Jersey, and his mammy's Ole Speck.

"His hair is jist es soft an' es fine es split silk;
I'll let 'im run out an' have all of her milk,
An' then, he'll improve all my cattle, ye know."
"Well, yes," says I, "Jeff, that is shore to be so."

The yearlin,' he growed and got powerful fat,
An' is hide were es slick es the Parson's new hat;
His horns set es purty as purty could be,
An' the beatenes' neck that ye ever did see.

One day, 'twere along 'bout the middle of June,
An' I were a smokin' an' takin' my noon—
I looked an' seed Jeff come apokin' along,
An' I knowed right imejitly sumthin' were wrong.

"Come in—have a chair—been to dinner?" says I.
"I've been through the motion," says he, mighty dry;
"But as shore's ye're borned, it's a mighty poor eat,
When a feller's got dinged little bread an' no meat.

"That yearlin' is not near so fine es he wus;
His hair it aire sorter beginnin' to fuzz;
His neck aire so spinlin' he never can't fight;
His legs aire too long, an' his horns don't set right:

"He are gittin' to be—though I s'pose he aire sound—
The ugliest yearlin' on top o' the ground;
My crap's but half made, an' my store account's full,
An' it's do on short rashuns, or butcher that bull."

"Hol' on," says I; "Jeff, ye're in too big a haste;
To kill that bull yearlin' aire absolute waste."
"I know it; but I can't work 'thout eatin,' ye know."
"Well yes," says I; "Jeff, that aire shore to be so."

So this were the eend of Jeff's big specerlation,
Improvin' 'is stock with 'is big calkerlation.
They eat up 'is meat, used his tail for a cracker,
An' bartered 'is hide fur some salt an' terbacker.

Now this aire the moral, or else I'm mistaken:
Ye can't have fine stock till ye raise ye're own bacon;
Men's notions aire big when their stummicks are full;
It were skacety of bacon kilt Jeff Hancock's bull.

QUEEN MARY.

SUGGESTED BY A PICTURE OF LAURA BOWERS, AS "MARY, QUEEN OF SCOTS."

The rain beats on the window pane
  In monotone so dreary,
And 'neath the eaves the storm wind grieves,
As one by one I turn the leaves
  Of thy sad tale, Queen Mary.

Ah! loyal Scott, thy task is done;
  Through eyes grown dim and teary,
I turn to trace, on yon sweet face,
The beauteous lines of regnant grace,
  Of Laura Bowers's Queen Mary."

Rehearsing oft the story sweet,
  Of which I never weary,
I see again the young queen reign,
And gladly join th' applauding train,
  And cry "Long live Queen Mary!"

W'EN CRAPS AIRE SHORT.

W'en craps aire short an cotton low
Ther's shore to be a pow'ful snow,
  An' then hard times come in;
The meat gives out, the trains all stop,
An' folks can't git a speck o' sop
  To roll the'r taters in.

W'en craps aire short, and spesh'ly corn,
Ther's shore to be a baby born
  Along about the time
A feller feels his poorness wus'
And has to set aroun' and cuss,
  An' haint got nary dime!

W'en craps aire short guanner bills
Grow bigger than the rocky hills
  Wher'on ye spread the stuff;
Yer 'backer 'lowance comes so short
Ye're 'bleeged to chaw the ho' made sort
  An' use the stems for snuff.

W'en craps aire short yer store account
Runs up to sich a big amount
  It leaves ye 'way behin';
Ye almos' lose yer confidence
In Scripter an' in Providence,
  An' all of human kin'!

W'en craps aire short you can't atten'
Yer church—no use in meetin', then,
  To try to make a spurt;
Ye can't show out ye feel so slack
With britches patched, an' to yer back
  Ye've sca'cely got a shirt!

W'en craps aire short ye lose the use
Of all ye knowed afore, so loose,
  Can't even try to l'arn :
Ye scol' yer wife an' buse yer frien's,
The bag to hol,' open at both en's,
  An' life ain't wo'th a darn !

THE WOODS.

DEDICATED TO THE FORESTRY CONGRESS OF 1888, AND READ BY
LOLLIE BELLE WYLIE.

The woods, the woods, the grand old woods
 That stretch o'er hill and dale and plain :
Oh, how I love the solitudes
 Of Nature's free and fair domain.

'Tis sweet, so sweet, the sun to greet,
 When every bough is gemmed with dew,
With odorous blooms beneath my feet,
 And o'er my head the boundless blue.

Each sturdy oak on feebler folk
 A benediction from on high
In loving kindness doth invoke,
 As through its leaves the south winds sigh.

The towering pine to heights divine
 With inspiration thrills the soul,
And points to where in splendor shine
 The stars that mark my spirit's goal.

The shadows fall from cypress tall,
 And cedar dark and sycamore,
Gnarled elm and ash, that oft recall
 The half-forgotten days of yore.

At Summer noon, when airs of June
  In idling dalliance fan my brow,
How sweet to hear the brown bees croon
  Low rythms around some blooming bough.

In Autumn time, when vespers chime
  And wake such pensive melodies,
With earth sublime in pictured rhyme,
  How glorious are the dear old trees.

When gaunt and grim each leafless limb
  Shrinks shivering in the wintry b'ast,
I gaze adown the vistas dim
  Upon the shadows of the past.

Then on the scene, some evergreen
  A ray of hopeful promise throws.
Its constancy and faith serene
  Brings to my weary soul repose.

The woods, the woods, the wondrous woods,
  Where all life's purer fancies dwell;
Where silence of the ages broods
  O'er dreams no mortal tongue may tell.

And truant brooks through shadowy nooks
  Flow from the noisy world apart;
With lore not found in sages' books,
  Their mystic murmurs fill my heart.

I love the woods, the haunted woods
  Where untold pleasures are concealed,
Where no discordant note intrudes,
  Where God and Nature are revealed.

When I am dead, may I be laid
  Deep in some wild and wooded dell;
Let forest treasures deck the bed
  Of one who loved them all so well.

A MESSAGE.

From the scene of my sadness, my dearie,
    I'll send you a message to-day,
Though the skies be darksome and dreary,
    And the world so cheerless and grey.
I'll release my dream-ship from its moorings;
    From this harbor of sorrows set free,
My spirit shall seek in its soarings
    One glimpse of the sunshine and thee!

In fancy I'll walk there beside thee,
    And breathing the fresh salt sea air,
I'll gather the blossoms that bide thee
    To twine in thy sunny brown hair.
I'll hear that sweet voice like a blessing,
    And thirstily drink each low tune,
And feel the soft, tender caressing
    Of that gentle hand in my own.

And oh, let me breathe in this message
    The longing that throbs in my breast,
And may its sad plaint be the presage
    Of years of contentment most blest,
When the days of my conflict are over,
    And the nights of vain watching are past.
When the heart beats of loved one and lover
    Keep time to life's music at last!

Hark! Mingled with chimes of the vespers
    Old Ocean is chanting, and hear
Faint and afar the low whispers
    Of hope that I breathe in your ear.
And borne on the night-wind's soft sighing
    Warm kisses for one that I miss,
And love and devotion undying
    In the touch of each passionate kiss!

CHILD OF THE CONFEDERACY.

ADDRESSED TO MISS WINNIE DAVIS, ON THE OCCASION OF HER
VISIT TO GEORGIA, IN COMPANY WITH HER FATHER,
HON. JEFFERSON DAVIS, MAY 1ST, 1886.

Fair daughter of a kingly sire !
Nurtured amid the fiercest fire
  Of battle's stern array ;
Thy lullaby the cannon's roar,
Or war note wild, of those who wore
That stainless garb of grey.

Too young to heed the mournful knell
Or feel the shock when Richmond fell,
  And the star of hope went down ;
But now the brightest, purest, gem
In that illustrious diadem—
  A throneless monarch crown !

Each throbbing breeze that gladly sweeps
Adown our rugged mountain steeps,
  In generous rivalry,
Hastens to bear the truest proof
Of homage rendered in behoof
  Of Georgian chivalry.

The memories of these gallant men
Run back to that dark season when,
  In chains, the conquering powers
Bore our loved leader far away ;
But, ah, we bring him back to-day
  In gyves of fragrant flowers.

Fear not to clasp each rough brown hand,
For gentle as they're brave these grand
  Old veterans of the war ;
Tho' each hath grasped a saber hilt.
And fruit of many a bloody tilt
  Each bosom bears a scar !

With Stuart's peerless band they bled,
Or marched where Stonewall Jackson led
  His victory-winning host;
And wept with Lee, when in defeat
Each warrior, rather than retreat,
  Fell bleeding at his post.

Unflinchingly they bore the brunt
Along the weary battle front
  In those wild days of strife ;
And for each thread of silver now
That glistens on thy father's brow,
  These men would pawn a life.

A prosperous people now, and free,
To Georgian soil we welcome thee,
  Storm-cradled child of Mars!
These guns are they that loudly boomed
'Round thee, best cherished bud that bloomed
  Beneath the Stars and Bars!

A thundering chorus welcoming
Attests the tribute that we bring,
  Instead of war's alarms,
With gifts of love within our gates,
The Empress of the Southland waits
  To fold thee in her arms !

DESPONDENCY.

Heartsick, dispirited,
Sorrow inherited,
Suffering unmerited,
Burdens so heavy and anguish unknown,
Sadly the wanderer
Walketh alone !

Walketh alone in the midst of the throng,
Who gladden the world with gay laughter and song ;
Looketh on pleasures, yet claimeth no part ;
Walketh alone with a pain at his heart.

"PO JO" IN AUTUMN.

(Suggested by the poem, "Po Jo," by Orelia Key Bell.)

* "Po Jo!"
Drooping with plumage all ruffled and rumpled,
'Mid blackened November leaves, withered and
    crumpled,
Pipeth pathetic, sad hearted is he—
"Joreter, joreter, joreter, joree!"

"Po Jo!"
Dog fennel milkweed, all
Dead and decaying,
By the stark thistles tall,
Chill winds are straying;
Prone on the sodden ground
"Po Jo" is lying, dying!
O'er the fields Autumn bound
Gray locks aflying;
None to caress him,
For walketh no more
She that would bless him
With the smile that she wore!
Waileth so wearily, weirdly—ah, me!
"Joreter, joreter, joreter, joree!"

"Po Jo!"
Dark clouds are drifting
Above the long sweep
Of the hills that are lifting
Bare brows to the deep
Sunless heaven, whence shifting
Gaunt shadows that creep
Down earthward to weep
In the drear solitudes
Of the death silent woods,
Lonely and longingly over the lea—
"Joreter, joreter, joreter, joree!"

* "Po Jo" is a ragged wild flower that infests Southern fields.

"Po Jo!"
Mournful the strain
Of the low sobbing rain,
And the echoes that chorus a dismal refrain,
Sorrow and sadness,
And the longing and haunting and hungering pain;
Anguish and madness
For the joy that will come not to gladden again!
And so often recalling
When twilight is near
That the light footstep falling
No more shall he hear,
Pensive and plaintive from yonder bare tree.
" Joreter, joreter, joreter, joree ! "

"Po Jo!"
When springtime returns,
And the delicate ferns
Peep shyly by banks where the wood violets blow;
And blithesomely burns
The star of the evening, and the West is aglow;
And wild roses bloom
In the soft, tender gloom;
Again wilt thou come,
Down-trodden and dumb,
"Po Jo !" all the taunts
And upbraidings to bear
Of the Mayweed that flaunts
Her gold-powdered hair,
And the insolent dog-fennel, base-born andlow:
None hath compassion or pity on thee !
" Joreter, joreter, joreter, joree ! "

"Po Jo!"
Grieveth the wind in the valley, and lone
The sighs of bare branches, the river's low moan ;
Somber the garments the dark mountains wear,
Murk as the gloom of a hopeless despair :
Sad as the pain-burdened heart that I bear!

The spring may return, but the sunshine will bring
No brightness to me, and the wild birds may sing
When green boughs are weighted with odorous flowers,
And dream-bells are tolling the long drowsy hours:
Far dearer to me
Than each dew-laden blossom!
A withered late violet
That died on her bosom.
Tearfully, tenderly touching—ah, me!"
"Joreter, joreter, joreter, joree!"

A GIRL OF ST. AUGUSTINE.

Along the narrow, winding street,
I stroll with half reluctant feet,
Where sunbeams struggle with the gloom,
Heavy with fragrant orange bloom,
Where feathery palm and clinging vine
And waving strands of moss entwine,
And happy birds their songs attune—
Spring's hopeful lays to airs of June.

Through spreading oaks and cedars tall,
A glimpse of lichen-covered wall;
Proud mansion, once, of some great dame
Of old Castilian birth and name;
Upreared in bold Menendez' time,
When Augustine was in its prime—
A fragment, now, of history's page,
Relic of some forgotten age.

But through the narrow casement high,
Whose arching roof shuts out the sky,
I catch a glance of melting eyes
With soft and languorous glow that vies
In splendor with the radiant light
Of brightest stars that shine by night,
When the last film of mist is driven
From off th' unclouded brow of heaven.

Beneath a crown of shadowy hair,
A maiden's face, divinely fair—
On brow and cheek, in sweet repose,
There blend the olive and the rose;
A neck as white as virgin snow,
Whose proudly curving outlines show
That through each lightly-penciled vein,
Still throbs the haughtiest blood of Spain.

Enraptured, there I stand and gaze;
My heart beats fast in fond amaze,
Till bird and blossom, vine and tree,
Are lost in silent ecstacy!
'Tis gone.   A stranger's ardent look
Her modesty could never brook;
But bears my heart its deep impress—
That dream of perfect loveliness.

Ah, lady! Dared my fond desire
To'ard heights sublime as they aspire—
Dared idly dream thy window there
The faintest ray of hope might wear,
At twilight hour would I return
To watch that kindling taper burn,
And wake such chords as well might move
Thy soul to hear my tale of love!

RAGGED REMINISCENCES

ATLANTA ENG. CO.

SOUTHERN SCENES.

PONCHARTRAIN.

Grandpa was the best man I ever saw but he had some exceedingly peculiar notions.

One of his funny habits was the way he named things.

His favorite little darkies had to grow up under the burden of such tremendous names as "Thaddeus of Warsaw," "Carl of Copenhagen" and "Lord Delaware."

If a mule was to be named, Grandpa would hang an appellation like a mill-stone about the neck of the quadruped.

Once he became the proud possessor of a clay colored puppy, and in spite of the earnest expostulations of the family, he insisted on naming that unfortunate descendant of a half dozen different breeds of dogs, by the high sounding title of "Ponchartrain."

Well, we got even with him, for when that puppy became a pot-bellied burlesque on his mongrel race, we shortened the name to "Ponch," and it was so excessively appropriate that it used to make me laugh in my sleep.

All about the plantation you could see this pair. Grandpa was very, very fat, and Ponchartrain took after him and kept after him till he got the very waddle of his portly master.

Hot summer days Grandpa would absent-mindedly walk off from the house without his shoes, and he would visit the watermelon patch and go around thumping them, chuckling to himself and making comments to Ponchartrain.

Suddenly he would come across his own track and it would look like where a mule had wallowed, and he would pause and examine it carefully.

"Ah, Ponchartrain, there's no devil if some nigger hain't b'en in here. Come here, Ponchartrain, phew-ew! Phew-ew! Good boy! Smell his track Ponchartrain! Sooboy! We'll catch up with that thievish marauder!"

Ponchartrain would flap one ear and gaze intently at the hole in the ground, and then he would look up in his master's face and whine, and Grandpa would encourage him.

"Go it, me boy! Sick'im Ponchartrain! You got the blood in you. Just a leetle more practice and you'll be the finest nigger dog in this beat."

Then Ponchartrain would whine and wag his fat tail, and begin to paw in the sand in search of a doodle.

But one day Grandpa and Ponchartrain got into a scrape.

The yellow-jackets had taken up their lodging in an old stump in the big new-ground, but Grandpa hadn't found it out. I knew, for if there was a yellow-jacket or guinea-wasp nest in a mile of the plantation, I always found it out right speedily.

Grandpa was out there about three o'clock one sunny afternoon to see how his pumpkin patch was thriving. The place was a very rich piece of ground, and the vines grew luxuriantly. It looked powerful snaky, but Grandpa always boasted that he was not afraid of snakes. He said that only drunkards and hypocrites need fear serpents.

A spreading adder had bitten him on the toe once, and the toe being so tough that the snake made no impression, I think that emboldened the old man.

He said that Ponchartrain was not afraid of snakes because he was double-dew-clawed, and snakes could not hurt dogs that were double-dew-clawed.

The sun beat down fiercely, and the sweat hung in beads on the old man's ruddy brow, and Ponchartrain had his tongue out.

Suddenly there was a rustle among the pumpkin vines, and a great brownish-black head was thrust upward, and two glittering eyes regarded the approach of the intruders with a look of surprise and indignation.

It was the old brown coach-whip that had been the terror of my waking thoughts and the prime factor in my nightmares for several summers.

"I—yi! You old son-of-thunder!" ejaculated the old man. "See 'im Ponchartrain? Sick 'im boy! We'll settle with the old villyun right now. 'The seed of the woman will bruise the serpent's head,' saith the scripter. Go for 'im, Ponchartrain!"

But Ponch was not in a fighting humor, and he drew back betwixt the old man's legs, and the latter turned to pick up a runner oak root, simply remarking:

"Well, I s'pose I can finish the old—Great Jewhillikins! Yeow-oo!" he yelled as something that felt like a coal of fire struck the plump calf of each leg simultaneously, and the old man fetched a leap, tripped over the dog and fell flat of his back, and the coach-whip went skinning across his legs like a streak of lightning.

It was hard to tell which scrambled to his feet first, Grandpa or Ponchartrain, but when they rose they rose running, and in their rear the pumpkin leaves quivered in the sun like the water in the wake of a pair of porpoises.

I was sitting in the shade of the mulberry tree as they came puffing and blowing by, and I saw Grandpa's hat and the big bandanna that he carried in it, as they floated away, and, oh golly! how I laughed.

Grandpa jumped the bars, and Ponchartrain wiggled through a crack, and as they went tearing down the lane the dust rose like a cloud.

Parson McCook was riding toward them on his moon

eyed mare, and she suddenly awoke from her reverie, and wheeling about, went flying away at the head of the procession.

I gathered up Grandpa's hat and his bandanna, and then I went on toward the house and rescued Parson McCook's hat and his saddle-bags, and just as I reached the steps, the parson came riding up to the gate.

"Light, light, Brother McCook," said the old man, as he shifted from one foot to the other; "ye see I have been atryin' to get my dog in practice to run the niggers out of my watermelon patch, and we had a purty tight chase of it, but I beat him a fair race. Here, Ponchartrain, come here, puppy."

But Ponch was hidden in the tea weeds, and there he stayed till he heard the dishes rattling for supper.

GRANDPA'S NEW YEAR.

Grandpa was a very industrious man.

Had he been as economical as he was industrious, his posterity would never have been forced to edit a weekly newspaper.

The only thing he was ever economical in was his industry.

But he was a very industrious man.

His industry was of that painfully intermittent variety that always robbed a Saturday afternoon in the midst of the bream fishing season of all its sweets, and turned a holiday into a day of disappointment and gloom.

He had a queer superstition, which he pretended was handed down from Benjamin Franklin, or some other worthy of cranky notions. It was that if you did a good day's work Monday you would get there every day during the week, and if you spent New Year's in idleness, you were sure to lose a great deal of time during the following Anno Domini.

In living up to these notions he caused himself much unnecessary and unprofitable labor, and made me suffer divers disappointments and sundry inconveniences that hang like mill stones about the neck of my most cherished memories unto this day.

For instance, he would forget all about that Monday work until Saturday dinner, and then he would suddenly remember it, and would say: "Well, my son, it is never too late to mend, so we will attend to that work now, for if we lose Monday's work we are likely to lose the week."

Then the sawyers, that I had so diligently sought by skinning a dozen pine logs, with which to entice the shy sun pearch and the blue bream, had to dry up and wither in the bait gourd while I delved and toiled at some Monday task that had been laid over until Saturday evening.

And just as sure as I laid up to enjoy a New Year's day, just so sure did that industrious old gentleman knock all my plans into flinderations.

One time, I remember well, New Year came on a sunshiny day, with the blue skies full of glorious light, and the crisp air burdened with joy bells of promise, and I awoke with pleasant anticipations of a perfect winter holiday.

We had planned a big rabbit hunt, and the dogs had been kept in training, and I had cut off Ponchartrain's rations for a whole week beforehand, so that he could stand a show with those long, hungry, flop-eared hounds of the Webb boys, that would lie down and roll over on a rabbit track three days old, and yell as if their hearts would break, and then get up and run forty miles in forty hours with a long-drawn howl at every jump.

All the morning I spent in fixing up for the hunt. Uncle Mose had made me a blowing horn out of the right horn of the Jimmerson bull, and he had polished it up as slick as glass and fastened a long, white buckskin string to it, so that I might sling it over my shoulder.

I spent several hours in the back yard trying to learn how to blow the horn, and I had tied Ponchartrain to the big locust tree, so as to train him to the sound of the horn.

When I would wind a blast Ponch would look up at me in a pathetic sort of way, and toward the end of the seance I thought that dog looked real unwell.

I would have forgotten all about dinner, but for the fact that Grandma sent Hetty, the house girl, out there to see if the motherless yearling had got his head hung in the fence. When Hetty reported that it was me practicing, the rehearsal came to an abrupt conclusion.

At the dinner table Grandpa suddenly leaned back and said :

"Well, my son, this is New Year's day. You know if we do a good day's work to-day we are likely to keep it up all the year ; but if we spend it in trampoosing around, we are likely to idle about and do nothing all the balance of the time."

"Dat's so, boss, de Lawd knows," ejaculated Uncle Mose, who was standing just outside the door. He was a deceitful old hypocrite, and didn't want to work any more than I did, but the hope of a dinner induced him to sanction Grandpa's statements.

"Hey, is that you, Moses? Give him some dinner, Hetty ; you know this is New Year. And Moses, just as soon as we get through we'll go on over the creek and get some timber for axe helves."

"Desso, boss, an' tankee, sah. I's wid you, sho's you bo'n."

And I gazed longingly at the new horn hanging on a nail, and thought how much I was going to lose on that rabbit hunt.

After dinner Grandpa bustled about and got the axe, and Uncle Mose got a maul and wedge, and I was told to bring along a couple of gluts, and away we went. It looked like a funeral procession. Grandpa led the way, discoursing at great length on the profitableness of labor and the beauties of industry, and Uncle Mose followed close behind, trying his best to step in Grandpa's tracks, and keeping up a string of

"Desso's," and "Adzackly, sah's," and "Dat's w'at I says,'' and all such agreeable answers that served to mollify Grandpa and increase his respect for Moses.

Next came myself, burdened with hopeless disappointment, and wishing that Uncle Mose had the rheumatism and that Grandpa had to go to court that day. Behind me, with nonchalant air, and listless eye, and drooping tail, and wagging ears, came Ponchartrain, without any special mission, a simple looker-on in Venice.

Suddenly a bright thought occurred to me. I knew where the bumble-bees had gone into winter quarters at the root of a fine young hickory tree, and I knew furthermore that this sunny weather would stir the blood in their torpid veins, and cause them to polish their stingers for the summer campaign.

I peartened up my gait, and getting close to Grandpa, I said eagerly:

"Grandpa, I know where there is the pur—tiest hick'ry tree you ever saw. It's the very thing you want."

"I yi, my son, show it to me, and I'll see what you know about axe-handle timber."

"Dat's so. Sma't chile dat is. Mek 'e ma'k some er dese days, sho's yo' bo'ned.

I led the way to where the tree stood, near the bank of the creek, and when Grandpa saw it he shaded his eyes with his hands and looked at it critically from top to bottom. Then he walked around and examined it from every side.

"Moses, the boy is right. It's the very dinktum, eh?"

"Dat's so, de Lawd knows, boss, an' it's des as I say: dat's de sma'test boy in dis diggin's. Mek 'e ma'k some day, sho's yo' bo'ned; bet yo' dat he shakes hands wid de gov'ner yit."

"Moses, what do you think of getting a maul out of the butt cut?"

"Dat's de t'ing, de very t'ing, boss; des dig 'em up by de roots, an' ye got 'em, sho. Oh, I tell ye, dat chile's got sense."

So they began to work. The soft, mellow loam was easy to cut, and Uncle Mose chopped all around with the axe, and then began to grabble the dirt away from the root of the tree. Grandpa sat on a stump to give directions, and Ponchartrain sat on his haunches, as he intently observed Uncle Mose's proceedings.

I withdrew a few steps in search of sparkleberries, for I had a premonition that there would be lively times around there presently.

"Hi!" cried Uncle Mose, stopping short and assuming a listening attitude. "W'at's dat?"

"What's what?" said Grandpa.

"I heah sump'n 'zoom-m in dar. Spec its er snake."

"Tut, tut. It's just the water in the creek. Go ahead, Moses."

Ponchartrain shifted his position, sniffed the air and whined.

"Be quiet, sir," said Grandpa. "What's the matter w—"

"Wow-ow! Oh, Jesus, marster! I'm snek bit!" and with a yell Uncle Mose jumped up and down, and with a roar like the rush of many waters the bees burst forth.

One struck Grandpa in the burr of the ear just as another plumped against his chin, and he tumbled off that stump and rose running.

"Kerslosh!" I heard him hit the water, and in a moment I heard Uncle Mose as he plunged in after him.

I made a dash to catch up with the procession and see the fun, and I got there just time enough to see Ponchartrain land squarely on top of Grandpa's bald head as it popped up, and to catch Uncle Mose's "Jesus, marster!" as he went under.

I was screaming with laughter, and ready to die, when a bumble-bee took me in the back of the neck, and in I went on top of Uncle Mose, who spluttered "Jesus, Mar-ar-sh—" as he disappeared again.

Finally we crawled out on the opposite bank, and I scrambled through the thicket and came to the open field.

It was the most woe-begone looking party you ever saw.

Grandpa's left eye was closed, and his nose looked like a frost-bitten potato. Uncle Mose's under lip hung down like a half-cured ham, and Ponchartrain's head **was** as big as a bull dog's.

The sun was low in the west and a cold wind was springing up.

"Going to be searching weather," said Grandpa, after we reached the lane and were nearly home.

"Dat's so, boss, an' de Lawd knows hit don' hatter s'arch fur ter fin' us."

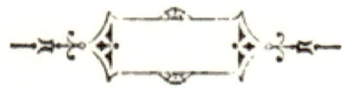

When I was small and young (and I always was smaller than I was young), I think I passed through some as tough experiences as most tow-headed boys do.

Right here let me say a word of encouragement to tow-headed boys. Their heads will not always be that color, for mine is now getting grey very fast. Then boys, ought not to grieve about whiskers. I did, and now it costs me ten or fifteen cents a week, according to the quality, to get a shave.

I used to be the cow-pen boy, and no boy who has had to serve an apprenticeship as a cow-pen boy in the flat woods will ever pine to go West and become a cow boy In fact, he will never want to be any other sort of a boy any more.

Oh, I used to have to paddle round on damp and drizzly evenings, when the toads and frogs were conducting concert more dismal than a Salvation Army pow-wow; and their "squa-a-n-k!" and "squo-o-n-k!" came in croaks and squawks from every puddle.

Then I'd have the ground-itch, and my toes would crack open, and I'd pour hot tallow in them and cut up all sorts of shines. Of all the concentrated essences of the most exquisite good feeling on this earth, scratching the ground-itch is the *ne plus ultra*.

We used to have a variety of remedies that I would love to give you the benefit of now, but I guess this generation never suffers such tortures as we did. Gourd vines, salt water, red oak ooze, and all sorts of queer compounds were used with varying success.

When great, gaping seams opened in our heels, we had a

way of greasing a piece of woolen string, slipping it into the crack, and then wearing it until the place healed over and the ends of the string wore out, and in these heels of mine there is now enough woolen yarn to knit a small pair of socks.

Cow-penning time was the bane of our lives. It was hunt the cows of an evening, and hunt the calves of a morning, and we were ever in search of something which explains, in part, that yearning, hungry look in the eyes of we sons of crackerdom.

Mother had an old cow called Calico, and that cow cost me more than the world can ever know. But for old Calico I might have been president, or I might have been in charge of a fat judgeship, or I could at least have ridden the circuit.

But let by-gones be by-gones. I have forgiven her.

One time, however, I got even with old Calico.

Mother thought there was no cow so gentle and placid as old Calico. I knew that her gentleness was laziness and her placidity was deceit. That old cow would stand behind a clay root and chew her cud for half an hour when I was hunting high and low for her, and then, when at last discovered, she would look at me in a quizzical way that was maddening.

One dreary morning, in early autumn, I was ordered to go for the calves, and after searching about three hundred acres of wood and field, I succeeded in gathering the sad-eyed, woolly little wretches together, and arrived at the cow-pen full of guile toward the whole bovine tribe.

Mother began milking, and I had to mind the calves off.

One by one the patient kine stalked languidly in to be milked, and mother "so'ed," and "back-your-leg-ged," and managed to get all milked but Calico.

I had hit upon an idea. I had a pin in my hand fooling with my pet toe that had an aggravated case of ground itch, and I got to thinking and thinking and thinking.

My thoughts cogitated as to whether as big a thing as a cow could feel as small a thing as a pin, and I didn't much believe that she could, or even if she could, whether she would pay any attention to it or not.

Mother was milking Calico.

Calico was gentle.

Would Calico feel a pin prick?

If so, would she mind it?

No.

In the first place, she was too big to feel such a little thing.

Secondly, she was too everlasting lazy to pay any attention to it.

The time of action had arrived.

I was standing on one foot near the gap.

I changed on to the other foot a step nearer to Calico.

I was on the off side.

Mother was on the nigh side.

Here was the time for the solution of a scientific problem.

Should I miss it?

I whistled a bar from my favorite tune, "Cotton-Eyed Joe."

I moved a little nearer to Calico, and then I paused and pondered, and mother said, "So, Calico!"

Thinks I to myself, "I'll make you reap where you have not sowed if you are not entirely bereft of all sensibility."

I expected to simply startle her from her reverie. She shifted her cud and continued to chew with a long, rythmic movement of her under jaw, and her ears laid back contentedly.

I moved a step nearer, and could hear the "chu-r-r, chu-r-r, chu-r-r" of the flowing milk, and then mother remarked mechanically, "So, Calico!"

Painful was the moment of suspense as I reached out my hand and leant over till I could touch her broad hip, and then—!—!—!

With a wild bellow of surprise, pain and indignation, Calico raised herself on her fore feet, and I flew over the cow pen gap and fell with a dull thud among the wet potato vines ; the bucket shot up and fell on mother's head in an inverted position, and, choking with rage and warm milk, she gasped out "s-so-o, Calico!"

But Calico was tearing through dog fennels and jimson weeds like there was a whirligust of !gad flies at her heels, and the calf was doing his level best to catch up with her.

Then mother saw me.

"What did you do to that cow?"

"Nothin'."

"I know better."

"No'm, I didn't."

"Yes you did, come 'ere to me."

I had to snicker or burst, although I knew my doom was sealed.

"Yes-s, you're laughing, are you? I'il make you laugh t'other side of your mouth."

As I reached the top of the fence she collared me, and there was weeping and wailing and gnashing of teeth.

Ah me! At this distant day I can feel my legs tingle, but oh, my crackey! I got even with old Calico.

A FIRE HUNT.

Cold and drear was the aspect that greeted my eyes, as I sat upon the old draw-bars by the horse lot and gazed across the brown expanse of Blue Spring plantation. Wild gusts of wind swept the fields at brief intervals, dying away in a melancholy sigh, and succeeded by a depressing stillness, during which the eddying rifts of golden leaves of the old China tree banked themselves in the fence jambs. In the west the sun was setting, the only sign of his august presence being the faint glow of the dark and dull reddish tinge upon the banks of grey cloud that stretched across the horizon. The great pine woods to the eastward rose in shadowy gloominess, each bough and branch of the tallest trees fully outlined against the leaden sky. From the northeast came a flock of wild ducks, flying high, and directing their course to the more genial feeding grounds toward the southwest. Half a dozen cattle were standing in a crouching attitude in front of the draw-bars, their rough coats looking all the more shaggy from their drawn and pinched appearance. Now and then a yearling would bleat in a peculiar whining, long-drawn kind of a way, and the mother would answer in a subdued "mo-oo" that was a sad thing to hear. And the hogs were squealing plaintively, and in fact everything wore an aspect of desolation.

While I was standing in the lane, thinking of the pitiableness of the animals that must spend the night outside, I saw Uncle Mentor come out of the crib with a big basket of corn on his shoulder.

"Where are you going?" I asked.

"Gwine ter feed de fatt'nin' hogs. Wan' ter go wi' me?"

8

Of course I wanted to go. So away we went, down by the old persimmon tree to the potato patch, where a large number of plump hogs were rooting in the soft earth, or disporting themselves among the vines. Uncle Mentor began throwing the corn right and left and calling, "Goo-oop, goo-ooy, pig-goop," in the monotonous way he had, and here they came from every direction. Some would smell of the corn, then wheel about and kick up in a disdainful manner.

"Dat's des de way dey do. Er fat hog's de sassies' fing in de worl'. Dey don' squeal nudder. An' ef yo' let yo' hog squeal in de pen 'e sho' not to git fat. Look at dat ole sutty sow, da'; she des too biggity fo' any use. Nevah min', ole lady; yo' git fixed fo' long."

. Before we left, the old man picked up several large "nigger-killers" and put them in his basket. "Gwine ter have roas' tater ter-night, an' ef yo' come down ter my house I'll tell yo' 'bout'n er funny scrape ole man Dave an' 'e boss, Mars' Roderick, got inter one night sorter lack dis."

After supper I obtained permission to attend the seance. When I reached the cabin Uncle Mentor was sitting on a bench busily engaged in mending a basket. I watched him as he dexterously twisted the long whiteoak splits into shape, humming his familiar tune:

> "Oh, walk in, walk in, walk in I say,
> Walk in de pa'lah ter heah de banjo play.
> Walk in de pa'lah ter heah de banjo ring,
> An' watch de niggah fingah w'ile 'e pick it on de string."

Before the fire lay several big potatoes which, from time to time, he turned around, so that they might be thoroughly cooked without scorching.

"Now, tell me about the fire hunt, Uncle Mentor," said I, with boyish impatience.

"Fiah hunt, didn' yo' say? Oh, yes, well I done fo'got 'bout dat twel yo' mentioned it. Go dere in de co'ner an' feel in dat big gou'd, an' yo' fin' some groun' peas w'at I done had seasonin'. Yes, dat was er bad scrape, I tell yo'. Yo' see ole man Dave 'e wus Mars Roderick's right han' man. Ev'ywher' one go de yudder go. Mars Roderick 'e wus de beatenes' man ter fiah hunt yo' evah heerd uv. 'E in de woods mos all de time, an' Dave, 'e al'us went long wid 'e boss, 'e did, an' 'e was es good as 'e boss wus. I tell yo, w'at, 'e wus er good un. Mars Roderick 'e tuck'n built Dave er cabin out on de roadside, erway f'om de quatah, an' Dave an' 'e wife live out da' in gran' style. But dey bu'nt a hole frough de back sticks of de chimbly, an' Dave kep sayin' 'e gwine to fix it, but 'e didn't, an' bime by dey bu'nt nudder hole frough right side uv de fus one, an' neider one wusn't bigger'n an auger hole.

"One night, Mars Roderick an' Dave dey puts out in de woods on er fiah hunt, dey did, an' de night was dahk es pitch. By some means dey rambled 'round twel dey los' de way, and dey' wan't no stars to tell 'em wey dey wus, an' Mars Roderick, 'e say 'Dave, wey yo' reck'n we is?' Dave, 'e so smart, 'e say, 'W'y, boss we right back uv de new ground', wey I been gitt'n boa'ds.' 'No, we not,' Mars Roderick say, 'we must be down close to de big flat wey I built de hog pen.' F'om dat dey got to argyin', an' las' Dave 'e say, 'Boss, I know de way home. I got two big ole niggah-killer tatahs in de fiah, an' I'se hongrey, an' ef yo' des go de way I tell yo' we be home in no time.' Den dey started off, an' it 'gun to sorter mist er little, Las, dey cum ter er tree what been fresh cut down, an' dey bofe 'membered dat it was a rail tree at de back side uv de new groun'. Den dey bofe broke out in er laff, an' 'greed dat dey was right, an' wusn't mo' dan er mile f'om home. Den

dey walked erlong right brisk, Mars Roderick keepin' de
light in de fiah-pan mov'in' 'bout 'hind 'im so es ter shine
de deeah's eye, ef 'e happen ter run 'pon one.   Dey had'n'
walked mo' dan er hund'ed yards w'en Mars Roderick 'e
stop right short an' reach 'e han' 'round so, an whispah low
an' easy to Dave, "Han' me de gun.   We right close
tu de biggest ole buck in de range."   Dave looked erhead,
an' sho' nuff, right out da' wus de eyes, des es plain es
day, an' de deeah mus' be mighty close 'case 'e eyes show
wide erpa't.   Mars Roderick, 'e tuck de gun, 'e did, an
"bang!" went de gun, an' dem eyes des flew all to pieces,
an' somefin' des set up er squall dat yo' could er heerd er
ha'f a mile or mo', an' old Dave 'e broke off in de d'rection
uv de racket des er hollerin' an' say, 'Oh Lo'd, Mars Roderick, yo' done kill Patsy, an' ruint my 'taters w'at I had er
roas'in, fo' God!   Mars Roderick, yo' done kilt Patsy!'
W'en 'e dashed inter de cabin Patsy wus up on de table er
yellin' lack de Old Nick.

   "Patsy, Mars Roderick say, 'wey yo' hit?'"

   "Oh, Lo'd!   Boss, I hit right yere in 'de head, an' my
brains is comin' out."

   "Ya! ya! ya!   I can' he'p but laff w'en I fink about dat
scrape.   W'en dey got er light, dey foun' out dat Patsy,
fool lack, had des lay down wid 'er head to de fiah, des lack
er niggah, an' de tatahs was done cooked to er mush, an'
de fiah died down, an' Patsy went to sleep, an' was des er
snorin' er way.   Dave an' Mars Roderick, dey wus 'fooled
'bout wey dey wus, and dey see de coals uv fiah frough dem
holes in de chimbly, an' dey fought dey wus de deeah's eyes,
an' w'en Mars Roderick shot, 'e des scattered de coals, an'
ashes, an' de saf' tatah all over de ole fool 'oman, an' hit's
er wondah de shot had'n' ter hit 'er, but dey did'n', an' old
Dave, ole cuss, 'e got so mad 'bout losin' 'e roas' tatahs
twel 'e lack ter jump right on Patsy an' larrup 'er good
fashion 'bout it."

A DEADFALL.

Mother was a great lover of geese, not for their own intrinsic sake, but for the revenue derived from their feathers; and I always thought that the louder the goose cackled the deeper the place it occupied in her housewifely heart.

I was never partial to geese, and especially to masculine geese, for we had an old white gander that was the terror of my infantile existence. I have worn blue spots on my slim shins for many a weary day, inflicted by that gander.

Ganders never die. They may grow old and grey in sin, but dead ganders are as scarce as dead gray mules.

Well, that old gander was boss of the bone-yard, and he knew it, and he never missed an opportunity of showing his maliciousness toward me. If I sat in the crib door, shucking corn, and happened to hang my foot outside the door, first news I would know, that unrighteous fowl would fetch a dig, and I would get up rather sudden and surprised like, and stand on my hind legs and howl for a much longer time than it takes to tell this.

Through the crack of the worm fence, he assaulted my unprotected feet; and he lay in wait under the kitchen door-step, in the gloaming, and smote me hip and thigh.

I used to throw rocks at him, and lightwood knots, and corn cobs, and everything I could get hold of. I concealed minnow hooks in grains of corn and fed them to him. I prayed that forty million forked streaks of lightning might strike him under the left ear, but it all did no good.

His days were long upon the earth, and for ten generations, regularly every Spring, he had the plumpest goose of last year's brood for a mate; and he strutted around and snatched the tail feathers out of the younger ganders who dared pay any attention to her. When there were goslings he cut up and cavorted like the fowl fiend. (Copyright.)

I used to know a little song:

> "O, lookee, lookee, here,
> O, lookee, lookee, there,
> O, lookee, lookee, 'way over yander:
> For don't you see
> That old grey goose
> A-smilin' at the gander!"

I used to sing it, whistle it, hum it, and dream about it. The air was weirdly pathetic, and appealed to my inner soul.

Mother didn't relish the hymn, nor the tune, either, to any alarming extent, and she generally ordered me to get out the minute I began to pipe—

> "O, lookee, lookee, here,
> O, lookee, lookee, there—

and, like a dutiful son, I generally got out at once.

One day I conceived a project by which I might slaughter a whole covey of partridges at one fell swoop. I had been killing sparrows by setting a plank on triggers; and I argued that, if half a dozen sparrows were slain by a single plank, a whole host of partridges might be crushed by one fall of a shutter.

With me, to conceive a scheme was to put it in operation. That is how I came to get my heels locked behind my neck, and couldn't get them undone; but of this another time.

I went to the lint room at the gin house and secured a big shutter. It was so heavy that I could scarcely carry it; but by much toil and travail, I managed to drag it to the edge of the plum orchard where the birds used.

Carefully adjusting the triggers, I scattered bait in liberal profusion under the triggers, under the shutter and for a considerable distance around it.

Then with a malignant leer of prospective triumph I stole away on tiptoe, humming—

> " O, lookee, lookee, here,
>   O, lookee, lookee, there,
> O, lookee, lookee, 'way over yander :
>   For don't you see
>   That old gray goose
> A-smilin' at the gander ! "

The first day I went to see about my scheme I found some of the bait gone, but the birds were shy and would not come too near the formidable looking trap.

Next day I went, and still no sign. But that afternoon mother said :

" Son, I'm going up in the field to wring broom straw, this evening, and I want you to help me."

" Yes'm."

" Don't run off now, for I'm compelled to attend to it this evening."

" No'm."

" You be ready when I call you now, and don't fool around about it."

" Well'm."

But I thought I'd get a peep at my deadfall as I went, and when we came near the plum orchard I lagged behind and finally got on a stump so I could see it.

" What are you doing ? "

" Lookin' to see if my trap's down."

" Where's the trap ? "

" Yonder by the plum orchard, and—Whoopee ! It's down, and I bet I've got a whole drove of partridges," and I dashed off through the briars at the top of my speed.

Mother came on more leisurely, and I had time to take

in the situation before she came up, but I was afraid they were not all dead and some might get away. I jumped around when I saw the bait was all gone, and at last I raised the shutter carefully.

Horror, of horrors! As I peeped cautiously under it I saw the tip of a white goose feather, and honeyed expectancy turned to the gall of disappointment, and I wished I were dead and gone to Alabama.

Just then her majesty appeared on the scene.

" How many did you get?"

" Dunno'm."

" Haven't you looked?"

" Yes'm, but I didn't go to do it. I declare I did'nt," I whindled.

" Didn't go to do what?"

" To—to—to—"

She had raised the shutter and there lay that wicked old son of Belial of a gander cold in death. He was mashed as flat as a fritter, and he hardly knew what did it.

I lifted up my voice and wept as I felt a vigorous hand laid on the slack of my pantaloons, and then I hit the ground, " Kerblim!"

" You little rascal!" Her voice was thick with emotion. " Kill my geese!" She raised the shutter. "I'll teach you to kill up my geese!" " Kerwhop!" the shutter came down on me. " I'll make you set dead falls!" She was getting excited. " All you think about!" She had got on top of the shutter. " Always studyin' up some meanness!" Patter, patter, went her feet as she danced up and down on the shutter, and I felt like a house had fallen on me, and just as I got so flattened out I couldn't holler, the shutter was thrown aside, and grabbing that dead gander by the neck she wore his corpse out on me, and the feathers flew.

Next day I was sitting on the fence wondering if two snakes were to start to swallow each other what would happen, when I absent mindedly began to whistle—

> " O, lookee, lookee, here,
> O, lookee, lookee, there,
> O, lookee, lookee, 'way over yander;
> For don't you see
> That old grey—"

The memory of that tragedy overcame me, and I suddenly realized that the edge of the rail hurt me where I was sore, and the whistle died away on my lips.

A WILD HOG HUNT.

Sometimes—I may say very frequently—hogs would stray off into the river swamp while young and go wild. Within the impenetrable fastnesses of our Southern swamps they would increase and multiply to an alarming extent, and the plantation stock would become thoroughly demoralized by them, and they would get to be regular marauders, breaking into the cornfields at night, then tearing down corn and eating as much as they chose, when they would betake themselves to the swamp again.

Early on a fine morning about the first of October, Grandpa came out on the piazza and called for Mentor.

The old man was soon on hand, and, feeling that there was some new project on hand, I hung around to investigate the matter.

"Mentor, come here and get a dram. We'll have some rare sport to-day if Ponchartrain is in trim."

"Your bery good healt, sah," said the old man, as he swallowed the generous bumper of New England rum. "Ponchartrain is all right, boss; an' I bin thinkin' some time dat ef yo' wuz gwine to do anyfing 'bout dem hogs yo' bettah mak' 'aste 'bout it, fo' de time run off mighty fas'."

"Well, as soon as we get breakfast we'll go down to the river and see if we can jump any of 'em."

I pricked up my ears, for I knew that a wild hog hunt was up.

"Grandpa, couldn't I help?" I asked, thinking that I would be surer of gaining my point if I tendered my services.

"Help? Great jewhilikins! What could you do with a big wild barrow with his bristles up?"

" I don't know, sir, but I could carry the strings to tie 'em with."

" Ha! ha!" laughed grandpa, " That's a capital idea. Well, I reckon you can go, but Jake says you got scared at a 'possum under a clay root, and I consider you a poor soldier."

I retired in confusion, but I was on hand when Uncle Mentor harnessed old Beck to the lumbering cart, and grandpa, mounted on old Bill, his favorite riding horse, with his hogskin saddle with its low pommel, looked every way like a hunter to my unsophisticated eye. " Come on, Ponchartrain," and the dog leaped about and yelped for joy as the cavalcade rolled off down the lane. I sat in the cart behind Uncle Mentor, and plied him with various questions regarding the wild hog business, and he, grumbling good naturedly, entered into all the little details.

" A-h, chile! yo' do lack all boys; yo' wants ter know all 'bout men's wo'k 'long w'en yo' too little ter do it, an' des es soon es yo' gits big 'nough yo' gits too lazy, an' meks out dat yo' done fo'got how ter do anyfing. Lack ole man Jeff say w'en 'e see de monkey. 'E tuck'n say, 'e did: 'Hello! Bubbah, can' yo' talk?' An' de ole monkey 'e grin at Jeff, den Jeff he tu'n 'roun' an' 'e laff and say, 'e did: 'Ya! ya! ya! Bubbah, yo' no talk 'case yo' 'fraid yo' marsa put yo' to wo'k.' Hit's mos'ly des es Jeff say, too, sho's yo' bo'ned hit is."

" But how about the wild hogs?"

" Oh, bless yo' h'a't, well, dey des gits off a'ter de nice juicy aco'ns, an' de sweet pine mas', an' bimeby dey gits kin' 'er sullen, an' dey say goo-oo, guff! w'en yo' frows de co'n ter 'em, an' nex' fing yo' know dey done gone wil', an' sot up fo' deyse'l in de rivah swamp. An' I tell you' right now, don' yo' nevah put pen'ence in er hog w'at show de

white uv 'e eyes.   Dey same like er dish-faced mule—dey
gwine ter play yo' er trick, sometime, sho."

Just at this time we came to the edge of the river
swamp.   We called it the Half Moon Bluff, from the fact
that the sand ridge ran right up to the channel of the
stream, which left the swamp above and curved around
against the face of the hill in a beautiful crescent, entering
the swamp again about five hundred yards below.   Grandpa
had done fastened old Bill to a stout sapling, and Beck was
soon tied to a swinging limb, because she rubbed the bridle
off so bad, and then we started for the swamp.

About twenty feet below us flowed the beautiful wine-
colored water, and under the willows, across the stream,
there glistened a snowy sand-bar.

Where we entered the gloomy swamp a dry lagoon led
off between two solid walls of black gums, water oaks and
tupeloes.   In narrow places their interlacing branches met
overhead, shutting out the sunlight, and causing a soft
brown twilight that made the gnarled, knotted and water-
lined trunks of the trees appear beautifully fantastic.   The
blue berries of the black gums hung thick among the varie-
gated foliage, and the drooping branches of the tupeloes
bore great clusters of the green, yellow and scarlet fruit.
So pretty it was that I would bite one now and then, and
make a wry face at its sharp, acid flavor.

"Yere wey dey bin, boss, Jemini !   W'at er track.   Dis
must be dat ole black barrer w'at runned de boys out'n de
new groun' las' week.   De ole cuss lack ter tare up dat
little fiste uv Jake's."

"Yes, that's a big hog, boys, and we'll have some fun.
He has been here this morning, too, but he is lying up now.
Come here, Ponch !—hogs, boy, hogs ! Sick 'em, old man,"
and away went the dog on the trail.   But it was a cold scent,

and he got along slowly. This gave me an opportunity to watch the crested blue jays as they gossipped and chattered among the acorn trees, and the little, tiny, swamp canaries, with their puffy yellow bodies, and the little black hood tied coquettishly under their chins. As we passed a little pool an Indian pullet, a bluish-purple water bird that flits about like a shadow, perched on a branch in some thicket and poked its long neck out to investigate the surroundings. It seldom utters a sound, and its movements are as noiseless as a shadow. But its bright yellow eyes are always on the lookout, and you seldom surprise it. Then I saw a great horned owl with his speckled body perched bolt upright on the lower limb of a big tupelo, his horn-like tufts erect, and his near-sighted eyes staring down at us in evident perplexity. He turned his head slowly as we passed, keeping those solemn eyes fixed upon us, without moving his body at all.

"Ef yo' des wan' ter kill a owl don't was'in' yo' ammernetion ; des keep 'im tu'nin' 'roun' an' erroun', 'twel 'e git 'e head mos' clean facin' 'e tail, an' den des mak' er long leap, an' 'e try to foller yo' so suddint lack 'twel 'e brek 'e necks, so dey say," said Uncle Mentor ; but just then Ponchartrain became very active and set off through an almost impassable thicket of palmetto and brambles, and in a few minutes we heard the "Goff ! goff ! goff !" of a startled hog, and then old Ponchartrain barking furiously as he gave chase. We ran down the open lagoon, and arrived at a bend just time enough to get a glimpse of the great black beast with his long tusks, flapping ears and bristling hair, as he rushed from the covert, crossed the opening and plunged into the tangled swamp below. We all yelled at the top of our voices, and Uncle Mentor ran down toward the river, while Grandpa turned out so as to reach the open woods, and as he was too fat to run fast I followed him.

After tripping up over a thorny bramble that scratched my shins pretty badly, I emerged from the swamp just as Grandpa stopped to catch his breath and to send out a startling whoop of encouragement to Ponch, who was now baying the hog away down the swamp. Away we went, and in five minutes were in a little opening in the center of a dense thicket of thorny vines and bushes. Ponchartrain was jumping around the thicket barking, and we could just discern the dim outlines of the great, shaggy monster, and hear the champing of his muscular jaws and the deep growls from his muffled throat.

Just then Uncle Mentor came up from the other side, and cried, "sick 'im, Ponch, take 'im boy!" and threw a chunk into the thicket to attract the hog. Ponch made a wild leap, and with a harsh cry the game broke cover and ran between Grandpa's legs, completely upsetting him, and scaring me so bad that I shinned up a sapling and slid down again, while the hog and the dog were struggling together, filling the air with the wildest shrieks, yells, groans and snarls that ever startled the sleeping echoes of a Southern swamp. Uncle Mentor came to Ponch's assistance in a twinkling, and after a great tussle between Grandpa, Mentor, Ponch and the black barrow, the latter was vanquished. As they drew the last knot in the stout leather thong, and told Ponch to "be done, now," I decided I would descend from my lofty perch, and was terribly shocked when I found that in my excitement I had not climbed up the tree at all, but was sitting flat on a tussock, clasping the sapling in my arms as if my life depended on it.

Then they got a stout pole and placed it between the fastenings of his legs and his body, and by taking each

an end they succeeded in getting him to high land, and
then to the cart.

"Boss, see dis ma'k in 'e eah? I knows dis ole shote—
de very same little deb'l w'at we fought wus gwine ter die
wid de thumps three year ergo las' spring. 'Membah yo'
tole me didn't mek no diffunce wedder we ma'k 'im or no,
'case 'e die anyway, an' I say I gwine put 'em in er little
diffrent ma'k, an' 'ere h'it is, des like I tole yo'. Who'd er
fought de little w'ite-eyed scoun'l would er cut up devil-
ment. But hit's des luck, I say. Don' never trus' er hog
w'at show de white in 'e eye; 'e boun' ter go wrong."

"I guess we'll fix him now, though," said grandpa, and
then we entered the swamp again. But although we
hunted till dinner time we found no more, and had to
return with no other spoils than old "Blackie."

"Nevah min', ole fellah," said Uncle Mentor, as we
drove home, "yo' done cuttin' de big Ike 'mong de hogs
now. De nex' time yo' have is w'en yo' made inter sasse-
ridge meat fo' de res' uv us hones' folkses ter eat. Yo' be
ap' ter let de new groun' co'n 'lone atter dis, only es de ole
boss 'lowances yo'."

MALACHI.

Ah, the old log church!

With its long roof of clapboards, and the swag in the middle where the back bone had weakened, and the broad, shutterless door, and the puncheon steps in front.

Then the side door where the women went in, and the window at the back of the pulpit. And the rows of benches running crosswise, and down next to the pulpit, either side, rows of benches that ran lengthwise.

These were for the old folks—mothers and fathers in Israel—and the old women sat on one side and the old men on the other.

The Amen corner. Grandpa had his seat up there, and he wore the old bench slick sitting there listening to the sound of the gospel and raising the hymns.

The old man—sacred be his memory—owned much cattle. He pastured his flocks and herds from the Ocmulgee to the Flint, and from Stono, where the devil dropped his shot gourd; and old Pindertown, on the north, to the black swamps of the Okeefenokee, and the pimple hills of Ocopilco on the South.

He hunted his cattle over an area as big as the German Empire.

He carried a whip that you could hear a mile, and when he hollered "cow holler," the echoes reverberated from pine-clad ridge and the banks of reedy river, till you would have thought it was a regiment of whangdoodles sounding the charge.

Grandpa was very religious. He used to get formidably happy, and when he shouted he shook the walls of the old log house like Joshua and his ram-shorns on the plains of Jericho.

And he could talk at love-feast till the tears would trickle down the cheeks of the brethren like the summer rain on the furrowed brow of Signal Mountain.

When he prayed I always thought the good Lord paid some attention to him, for the old man meant every word he said, and he spoke out loud, and if he wanted rain he just asked for it.

Some of the rest of them I was a little doubtful about ; but I knew the good Lord was obliged to hear Grandpa.

I can see him now, raise himself, clear up his throat, and as the preacher finished "lining out" the hymn, the old man's broad chest would expand, a new light would come into that keen grey eye that was as sharp as an eagle's ; and—

> " All hail the power of Jesus' name,
> Let Angels prostrate fall."

Another pause while the next two lines were read and like the rich throb of some great organ—

> " Bring forth the royal diadem
>   And crown Him Lo-o-rd of All—
> Bring forth the roy-al di-a-dem
>   And crow-n H-im Lo-o-rd of All!"

Weaker voices swelled the grand old anthem of triumph, but Grandpa's voice led all the rest.

It was like the deep rich roll of summer thunder, accompanied by the rythmic patter of the falling rain.

I just knew then, and I have no doubt to this day, that angels gazed over the walls of paradise and chanted a joyous refrain.

I was a little Catholic. Too young to know much about it, and I looked upon Grandpa as my father in God.

And my confidence was not misplaced.

9

This very night, somewhere beyond the twinkling stars of heaven, the old man is wandering among perennial pastures and by streams that never go dry. And his great big heart is throbbing with calm contentment, and his great big voice is leading some choir of angel voices in that same old song—

"And crown Him Lord of all!"

One time, howbeit, the old man got me into a predicament.

It was one Sunday, when they had love-feast. Those wiregrass Methodists had real feasts of love in those days, when they laid aside the bickerings and cares and the fretfulness of earth, and gathered themselves to worship the God of love.

And the sun shone on leafy trees, and the winds were sweet and low as they sang softly among the pines. Wild birds flitted from wind-swayed bough to blooming thicket, and at the foot of the hill the streamlet crooned among the pebbles.

Far away in the golden deeps of the summer heavens cloud-ships lay at anchor, soon to hoist sail for the land of dreams.

One by one the elder members arose and told their experiences, and, good souls, magnified the few small sins their simple lives had known into black and bitter wrongs against their God.

Grandpa sat with his hands on the back of the bench in front of him, and listened with deepest interest to all that was said, now smiling gladly with one whose face beamed with the gladness of hope; now brushing off a tear in sympathy with some one whose anguish of spirit wrung scalding tears from a burning heart.

I grew drowsy. I had committed but few sins. Stole a

few watermelons, perhaps; or caused Ponchartrain to kill
the tabby cat's kitten; or broke up a bluebird's nest; or
told a story about going in swimming. But they were sins
too small for God or Grandpa either to mind much.

I sat on a crosswise bench where I could watch Grandpa
and keep my eye on the preacher, all at the same time.
Besides, I wanted to swap knives with Charlie Remington
as soon as they all got through, and the love-feast was of
only secondary interest to me.

Grandpa's time came.

I was watching a jaybird in an oak tree outside, and my
eyes were trying to make me believe there were two jay-
birds, when I knew there was but one. .

The old man arose, and resting his hands on the back
of the bench, he gazed away off in the distance for a
moment, and then cleared his throat.

"A-hem!'

He took the big red handkerchief from his hat by his
side, wiped his ruddy face, and another—

"A-hem!"

Then he began deliberately—

"Well, bretherin, I feel that we aire all sinful creatures
in the sight of God. The Scripter saith: 'He that saith he
liveth and sinneth not is a liar, and the truth aint in 'im!'

"But I don't b'lieve in puttin' too much distress on our
sins and shortcomin's. We're bad enough without that.

"Let us be of good cheer, and not be cast down. Our
Saviour tells us that He will send a Comforter, and 'if I go
not, the Comforter will not come.' I am mighty well satisfied to take His word in all these matters.

"He has gone to prepare us a home, but He has not left
us hopeless. That is the beauty of religion.

"And I want to tell you a source of great comfort to me.

You know for sev'ral weeks I've been a-ridin' in the woods and I ain't had much time to attend to my duties like I ort to, but I've kept my Bible with me, and I've been a readin' at odd chances

"And I want to tell you a little book that I've came acrost in the Bible that has done me more good than a little. And I want you all to read it keerfully. It's a little book away over in the back of the Old Testyment, and you mought miss it unless you looked close.

"Mind what I tell you, now, and 'tend to this right away. Fust thing when you go home, do you hunt it up and read it keerfully.

"Away out yander in them lonesome woods "—and one rough, brown hand was raised in the direction of the forest—"that little book has be'n a comforter to me.

"It is the little book of Malachi!"

Bang!

The fist came down on the back of the seat; I started from my doze, the jaybird flitted away, several old men groaned, and several old women said "Bless the Lord!"

The old man sat down.

"Malachi, Malachi, Malachi."

The name seemed imbedded in my memory like a bullet in a tree.

"Malachi."

All the day it haunted me, and at night I awoke from a dream and muttered, "Malachi!"

Next day I kept thinking over it, and it bothered me.

"Malachi."

I would look it up. Grandpa said it was good to read, and Grandpa knew. So I would make a still hunt for Malachi.

I found it, just as he said, and I read it over and over—skipped the hard names and spelled out the long words.

But to save my life I never was able to discover anything of special interest in Malachi. I found it very short, and I decided that was why he found it so comfortable. He could read it while his horse was eating, and be done with it.

And although I reverence the very wild vines that clamber over his crumbling tomb, and cherish every memory of the good man that is gone, I am still puzzled about Malachi.

Perhaps

> If I should live to be
> The last leaf on the tree

In the spring, I might find that comforter which the old man found in reading Malachi.

OLD PENNY.

Old Penny!

Ah, what mellow memories are awakened by the sound of that name!

My Uncle John was one of the best men I ever knew. He had Hardshell Baptist proclivities, was as honest as the day, and a jam-up man in every sense of the word.

But in the good old days he possessed the singular pecu-liarity of owning things that were small. He had the smallest ax I ever saw, his hogs were guinea, he grew little cob corn, and he owned Penny.

Away back, before the woods were burned, that little old mealy-faced mule was foaled. Her mother was a jenny and her father—well, he was some sort of a nondescript quadruped, and Penny was no bigger than a pound of soap after a hard day's washing.

Uncle John had a little two-wheeled cart, just the size for Penny, and when he hitched up and mounted Penny, the man and the mule and the cart looked like they were made for each other.

On a few acres of poor, pimply, pine land, that good old farmer with that little old mule made a good honest living and reared a large family of children, and the days of his life passed as quietly and calmly as if the great busy world were as far removed from him as the twinkling stars of the midnight sky from the drifting clouds of autumn.

One time they had a wedding at another uncle's house, and this event was to be very largely attended. Mother put on my little velvet coat and my new copperas and check breeches, with the galuses, and my copper-toed shoes and my cap that Uncle Jimmy gave me; and we started to the wedding.

She rode old John and I rode behind. The way was long and lonely, and my short legs got awful tired as we jogged along the lonely road among the whispering pines.

Past the cypress ponds, and across the Big Branch, with its wine-colored waters flowing over the sunny sands, and on into the big road we traveled.

I was not up in wedding matters, and I philosophized and speculated a good deal.

Old John pudged along with his ears flopping and his eyes half closed, and nobody would have dreamed that the old scoundrel cultivated a single evil thought.

As we came to a sharp turn in the road, with a thicket just ahead, suddenly old John fetched a wild snort, and wheeling around, he kicked up his heels and away he went, leaving mother among the gallberry bushes by the roadside; and I, unfortunate fellow, landed square on my nose, striking the hardest place in that hard road, and the world became illuminated by more stars than Gallileo ever dreamed of in his wildest imaginings.

And the cause of all the trouble was soon apparent. There, just in front of us, stood old Penny, with Uncle John a-straddle of her, and the little old rip was so allfired ugly that she scared old John out of his senses.

Uncle John was by our side in a twinkling, and mother was laughing, while I wept and wiped my crushed and bleeding nose. I think Penny actually smiled as she eyed old John, who was standing all a-tremble with fright, the old villain being too lazy to run far.

Uncle John caught him for us, and got us up again; but the wedding and all its prospective pleasures had no charms for me with my nose in a sling, and all because of old Penny. John evidently thought she was a ghost of some departed mule, for he would not pass her, and Uncle John had to lead her out in the woods till we got past.

Long afterward—after the war closed and my good old uncle came home to resume the quiet and even tenor of his uneventful life—he found that Penny was growing stiff in the joints, and his farm work required a younger and stronger animal.

But his heart's best affections were centered on the little old brindled mule that had grown gray in his service. He purchased a young mare, and broke her to the plow and the cart, but she had frisky ways that did not set well with the quiet old man, who was himself growing aged and worn with toil.

He kept Penny, although it was frequently suggested that he swap her. Finally the little old mule gave out, and one morning, when the old farmer went out to feed the stock, Penny was unable to get up.

Broadside she lay under the shed, with her dimming eyes turned pathetically toward the form of her kind master, who spoke to her as tenderly as if she had been a child instead of a poor little dumb brute.

The young mare was prancing and kicking up around the lot, and whinnying with pure wantonness, but the old man paid no attention to her gambols. The mists gathered in his eyes. He was thinking of the days long passed, when he came there to that wilderness of unbroken forest with his dark-eyed bride, a few head of wild cattle, and a few guinea hogs and Penny. His mind reverted to all the joys and sorrows that had lighted and shadowed his life. He remembered the grievous time when he reverently closed those dark eyes and turned to pacify his week-old baby boy, who was never to know a mother's love.

All these, and many more incidents and episodes of a

life of toil, passed through the old man's eyes as he watched the dying throes of the poor little companion of his labors, and as the last low sigh of departing life escaped from the quivering nostrils, the good old man turned away, and leaning against a fence he wept a few tears of sorrow over the close of the earthly career of the little mule.

And we boys all felt like one of the family had passed away, and we felt sad when we went by the empty stall and looked in and missed the familiar form of old Penny.

MY FIRST PAIR OF BOOTS.

Sweet are the memories of childhood.

No matter if that childhood were clouded with disappointments, memory bleaches the shadows and burnishes the sunbeams, and the farther away we get from it the brighter grows the picture.

Once Grandpa gave me a little frosty-sided calf that I loved as I loved myself.

Because her coat was of a beautiful pink and white color, and her tapering horns were ivory white, tipped with carnelian, I called her " Rose."

Oh, what a treasure that calf was !

I used to watch her feeding with other cattle, and she seemed to be the daintiest of the herd.

They licked up fennels, weeds and all in a gross and greedy fashion, while Rose only nipped the tenderest tidbits of green grass that grew among the violets and buttercups.

Among the coveted treasures of my boyish dreams was a pair of boots with red tops and shiny letters on them. The hope of possessing these haunted my dreams by night and troubled my thoughts by day.

But I could never secure enough cash at one time to purchase them, and I just went on plotting and planning, hoping and anticipating as the years rolled by.

Every Christmas I hoped to get a pair of boots for a present ; every birthday I looked with eagerness for some good friend to bring me a pair of boots.

I became so deeply imbued with the hope and longing for this one possession, that all my plans centered on that idea. All the pictures that I drew of future life had a pair of shiny boots in the foreground.

I used to look at prints of Napoleon in high boots, and I thought if I only had the boots, he might keep the fame all to himself.

One winter evening, when the wind blew sharp and shrill, and a raw mist hung over the hills, I heard a low "moo-oo" at the lot gate, and going out there I found Rose, shivering in the lane, and staggering around her was a little clumsy calf, just as near like Rose as it was possible for a calf to be like its mother.

Oh, how proud I was!

The big gate was flung wide open, and Rose was soon sheltered snugly, and a big basket of shucks and an armful of nubbins at her disposal, and the little old wobbly calf was curled up in a corner, sleeping like a kitten on a rug.

I was proud and happy.

Rose had a calf, and I had two cattle instead of one, and I valued that calf almost as much as I would have valued a pair of boots.

Winter hung on tenaciously that year. The chill winds of March kept the birds and the blossoms disheartened, and the cattle suffered severely.

But I looked after Rose and the calf, little " Dock," as I christened him, with the tenderest care.

I saw that she was turned into the rye patch every day, and I gave her shucks and nubbins every night.

And oh! how jealous she was of that little calf.

Did you ever notice the new light that comes in a woman's eyes when she looks on her first-born baby? There is something ineffably tender in the expression. The mingled hopes of a thousand love-dreams seem entwined in that look.

Do you know animal mothers are very much the same way? A cow can tell the bleat of her calf, or a ewe the cry of her lamb, among ten thousand.

I used to watch the fond, eager look of Rose, as she gazed on that calf, and imagine how much she loved him.

One evening in March the wind had been blowing pretty sharp, and there were a number of dead pines that had caught fire in the sap, and were burning fitfully, as the wind rose and fell.

At twilight Rose was not at the bars, and little Dock was fidgeting around, bleating piteously, and peeping through the bars in the direction of the field where his mother was accustomed to feed.

I got up on the fence and called aloud as the dusk deepened, but there was no response.

Finally, I went in search of Rose, but I failed to find her, and that night I was oppressed by such a strange foreboding that I could not eat my supper, and went to bed with a pain at my heart, for I could hear the little plaintive bleat of the calf, as he stood shivering in the darkness outside.

Next morning, ere the mist had lifted, I was out in the crisp air, racing away over the field in search of my cow.

Away down in a corner I noticed that one of the tall trees that was burning the evening before had broken off, and I could see a white something lying by.

I approached the spot with a sickening dread, for I felt that it was my cow.

As I came nearer, my worst fears were realized.

It was Rose!

A large limb had broken off when the tree fell, and struck her on the neck as she was feeding, and crushed her to the earth.

It was my first sorrow. I sat down on the charred log and wept bitterly.

It was just my poor, hard luck!

The only thing I owned that could look at me and love me was dead.

A film was over the soft brown eyes, and the hoar frost glistened on her pink and white coat.

I was alone with the dead.

Faint and afar I heard the wail of the weakling calf that had stood there at the bars all night, cold and hungry, waiting for the mother that would never come.

I turned away and walked slowly homeward. At the lot I stopped, and little Dock looked up at me pleadingly, as if he were asking me if I knew why his mother came not.

I tried to tell him, but my voice was husky, and I could only murmur hoarsely, "Poor little Dock!"

Choking with tears, I told Grandpa what had occurred.

The good old man was not as deeply moved as I, for he had seen death too often to be so touched by the loss of one cow out of the herd.

Then she was only a cow.

But with me she was more than that. She was different from all other cattle, because she was my very own.

At last Grandpa said :

"Now, I can tell you how to turn your loss to some profit. Get Abe to help you skin her, and you can have the hide to buy you a pair of boots."

This was a new idea. But there was a hard struggle in my heart. Rose had been my pet and my pride, and the thought of stripping off that coat which I had often stroked so fondly, and selling it for a price, was extremely repugnant. I felt that it was almost sacrilege.

All the morning I studied the matter over, and finally resolved to follow Grandpa's advice. It was the first triumph of practical common sense over sentiment.

Perhaps if there had been more such victories in my life, the current might have been materially changed; but alas! such victories have been few and far between!

As Abe and I passed the lot, I peeped through the bars, and there stood little Dock. His voice had grown weaker, and he looked at me with a dumb pathos that wrung my heart.

I stopped and considered a moment, and then I proposed to Abe that we try to feed the little orphan first thing.

Back to the kitchen we went, and Aunt Ailsie made us some gruel, and we then returned to where the little calf was, and after a long while succeeded in getting him to eat some.

Then we went about our other errand. I never experienced such a conflict of contending emotions before nor since.

Even now I cannot steel my heart to rehearse the sad details of that task.

At last the deed was done, and the hide was hung up to cure, but it was put where little Dock could not see it, for I felt it would be wickedly cruel to do a thing like that.

After we finished skinning the cow, we took it into our heads to bury her, and with the aid of several of the boys we dug a shallow pit and placed the remains of poor Rose in there, and covered her up, and left the rough mound to the changing influences of sun and dew.

We taught the little motherless calf to eat, and he soon began to thrive, but he never ceased to look for his mother, and I believe she wondered for a many a day why she did not come.

Every evening when the shadows lengthened he would stand at the bars and gaze across the darkening fields and bleat piteously.

At last I got a chance to go to town, with the wagon, and I carried my cowhide along.

I was pretty much of a stranger in town and my simple country ways used to cost me many a feeling of mortification.

As I shouldered my cowhide and walked over to Mr. Pardee's store, the boys all laughed at me, and I felt all broken up, but I was determined to sacrifice every feeling for the attainment of that one object.

Beside, what were the jeers of those town boys compared to the plaintive cry of little Dock?

I had gone through the ordeal of mutilating the body of the cow I loved so well, and now I felt equal to any emergency, for there could be no harder task than that.

Mr. Pardee was one of those chirping, cheerful little men, who pass the sunshine around on cloudy days, when all the rest of the world has the blues.

He met me with a ringing—

" Hello, my boy, what can I do for you?"

" I've got a cowhide, and I want a pair of boots," I stammered, stating my wishes in that concise style.

"Got a cowhide, eh? Wrong time o' the year for first-class hides. Is it a murrain hide?"

"No, sir; a tree fell on my cow and killed her, and I skinned her because I wanted a pair of boots."

There was a tremor in my voice that touched him. He eyed me a moment and said :

" All right, I'll see what I can do."

I thought to myself that he, too, had been a little boy sometime, and, maybe, had wanted a pair of boots as badly as I did.

"Just comes to one dollar and ninety-seven cents, but I'll make it two dollars," said he, as he weighed the hide and figured a little.

"Have you got any two-dollar boots?" I asked with a misgiving that I would miss my object, even after all my pains.

"N-o," said he, hesitatingly, "we have not, but I will see what we can do. Here's a pair for two dollars and seventy-five cents. You can have them for two sixty. Have you got any money?"

"No, sir; that is all I've got."

He whistled as he turned the boots over and over, and looked at me, then at the boots. His heart was undergoing a struggle, but not near such a one as mine was engaged in.

"All right," said he, suddenly, "you can take them any way. Pay me the sixty cents some other time. I know sorter how a boy feels who wants a pair of boots and lacks a little money to pay for them," and as he spoke he wrapped them up hurriedly, snapped the twine with a jerk as if he feared that his heart would fail if he hesitated, and as I walked out he turned away, whistling an uncertain air.

That evening when I got home, Grandpa admired my boots; Aunt Ailsie said I was "'mos' a sho' 'nough man wid boots on." The boys all examined them critically, and decided they were tip-top boots.

I wore them out to the lot, but in the failing light I saw a little white figure peeping disconsolately through the bars, and I heard that plaintive wail of hopeless longing.

It was little Dock.

I would have given all the boots in the world right then to have seen Rose come walking up the lane as of old, with the motherly look in her meek brown eyes.

I don't believe Grandpa was cut out for a trader.

If he was, he was spoilt in the making up.

There was a screw loose some way, for I noticed that he invariably got left when he undertook to swap anything.

He had purchased the gray mule, Jinny, when she was a three-year-old, and he had kept her thirteen years, but she had been so well treated that she even looked younger than she did when she was broken.

The truth of the business was, she never had been broken. She had just been bent.

She was as good as she ever was, only she had picked up a few extra tricks during her sojourn on the plantation. She had no idea of dying, for who ever saw a dead gray mule?

Grandpa liked old Jin, as we called her, although he never made any ardent display of his affections, from the fact that Jin was not the kind of a critter to be made up to.

There were certain peculiarities about her that made her an unpleasant and uncompanionable beast.

If you were riding along ever so nicely, and Jin took a notion that you were beginning to feel anyways stuck up about it, she would straighten that back of hers, stick both ears straight out in front, a slight quiver would permeate her frame, and you would think that the stars had fallen, and that you had fallen among them. She could throw a fellow the hardest fall and make him hit the grit more emphatically than any mule that ever walked the earth.

Then, if she didn't want to work to the gin or sugar mill, she would play off sick. She would creep up in the northeast corner of the lot and curve her tail out in an abject attitude, let her neck relax until her head dropped nearly to the ground, with her ears flattened out and her under lip hanging down, and she could be the sickest looking mule that you ever saw.

One day a man rode up to the gate and hello'd.

Grandpa was sitting on the piazza, and he got up and came to the gate.

"Good mornin'; got any swappin' stock?" said the man.

That is the way they used to do, without any ceremony.

"Ahem! Well, I don't make it a business to swap horses," said Grandpa. "What mought your name be?"

"My name's Jernigan. I'm from Telfair, nigh the Ocmulgee River. My business is hoss swappin', when I kin fin' the right kind of a feller what wants to live an' let live. Hain't you got a mule that you'd like to swap for the cr   in st saddle hoss in seven deestricts?"

"   n—Jernigan; lemme see, are you any kin to old n   hnnie Jernigan?"

"H   my own dear uncle, sir, only he's a better feller than I   fur a honester man never breathed the breath o' life t   acle Johnnie Jernigan, ef I do say it. Do you know ?"

     to know a man by that name when I hunted
     ork—"

     've got a stock o' cattle, have you? Well, sir,
     ry animal you're a lookin' fur. Whoa, Blaze,
     n to you. Ef we can't strike up a trade thar
     done. Watch how he can pace," and there-
     an rode off with a cluck toward the lot
     ranced back again.

     bar's the hoss fur you. He's too light fur
     a mule to break new ground with. But
     that aire hoss can travel! I've rid from

Burkett's Ferry, on the Lophaw, to-day, an' its nigh onto thirty miles, ef it ain't dang me, an' you see thar ain't a hair turned."

Grandpa eyed the horse and eyed the man, and fidgetted around. I could see that he liked the horse, and then, besides that, he wanted to get rid of Mr. Jernigan without hurting his feelings.

"I have thought about tradin' one of my mules for a good saddler," said Grandpa, "but I'm sorter careless about it."

"A fellow told me, what know'd you, that he thought I could git up a trade with you. Lemme see, what's 'is name?"

"Lives up the road here?"

"Yes."

"How far?"

"I dunno; three or four mile an' a half or so."

"Twarn't Welch?"

"That's the very man; that's him."

"What did he say 'bout it?"

"Said you had a mule you mought trade."

"Didn't say it was a gray mule?"

"Yes, that is jest precizely what he did say, now that I think of it. 'Twas a gray mule."

"Gray mule Jinny?"

"Adzackly. The gray mule Jinny. That's the very mule."

"Well, I hain't hardly made up my mind about swappin' that mule. She's done good service. She's been a faithful mule fur lo these many—ahem! I mean for several years."

"Purty old, is she?"

"No, she ain't so very old. I've got 'er exact age set down, som'ers."

"Whar is she?"

"She's in the lot. Go put the bridle on Jinny and bring her out, my son. Better take a shuck and brush some o' the dirt off, for them niggers never curry a mule if I don't stand right over 'em with a whip."

Grandpa knew that old Jin had been in one of her weaving ways that morning, and he knew that she had rolled in the mud until she was as dirty as a pig.

I went and got the bridle, and started to catch the old rip, but she knew that it was not work time, so she had straightened up her head and was standing on three legs, sunning herself, when I started toward her.

"Whoa, Jin," said I, but she jumped and snorted and turned her heels toward me.

"Whoa, you old heifer, you," and I let drive a wet corn cob that took her in the flank and made her kick up so high that she winked her left eye at me betwixt her fore legs. Then she came at me ringing and twisting and chewing her tongue, pawing and kicking, and I scaled up the gate post and yelled:

"I can't ketch this old fool. I'm scared."

"Goodness me alive! Jest like a boy," said Grandpa. "There ain't nothing the matter with the mule, only she jest feels good. Sorter coltified."

"She's old 'nough to know better," said I, spitefully.

"That's so, buddy," said Mr. Jernigan, with a snicker.

"She's not an old mule, Mr. Jernigan; you can see that, and she's got a lots o' sperrit about 'er. Whoa, Jinny."

The mule sidled up into a corner, backed her ears and said "wee-k."

"Whoa, Jinny," said Grandpa, soothingly.

"Purty wild, fur an old mule, ain't she?" said Mr. Jernigan.

"No, she's as gentle as a cat. Works well anywheres, and is a good saddler. I ought to know, for I broke 'er, an' I've owned her for nigh onto—I mean that was several years ago."

"She's got a dish-face. I'll bet she's got the devil in 'er."

"No, she hain't allers that way," I put in, "but she—"

"She's jest a little playful when she feels good." said Grandpa.

"Three white feet. Umph! Bad sign. Whoa, there. Lemme help you ketch her," and grabbing up a board Mr. Jernigan gave her a rap that made those heels glisten in the sun.

"Hold on, Mr. Jernigan, don't excite her. That's jest what's ruined—I mean that's what makes her a little hard to catch now. Them niggers—"

"Yes," said I, "Jim and Solomon had her up in a stall and put a running noose around her leg, an'—"

"Oh, it wasn't that bad. They jest said that to be a'sayin'," said Grandpa.

"Purty tough old cuss, ain't she, buddy?" said Mr. Jernigan.

At last they got the bridle on, and Grandpa started to lead her out. Just as he came to a mud hole he made a little jump over it, the old mule set back, and "kersplash!" he came down with both feet.

"Pick up somethin' and make her come on," said Grandpa to me, and I could see that he was doing his best to hold in.

I let drive another soggy corn-cob, and the old mule fetched a jump, and came down with all four feet in the mud-hole, sending a shower over Grandpa and Mr. Jernigan.

"Dam the beast!" said Mr. Jernigan, as he wiped his face, and Grandpa said:

"That's the only reason I would trade 'er, is because she is so full of sperrit."

"Stems her fodder, eh?" said Mr. Jernigan, rummaging in a feed trough.

"No; not old enough for that. You're in old Ben's stall; ain't he, my son?"

"Yes, sir; but they put old Jin in there last night, 'cause she was sick—"

"That's one thing about her—she can play off sick to perfection, when there ain't a thing the matter. That's the only trick she's got," said Grandpa, "and I thought I'd tell you, so if we swap, you won't be alarmed—"

Oh, I see she's colicky. Got a tetch o' the grubs, too, eh, buddy?"

"No, sir; Solomon says she bellowsed—"

"Sol don't know. Her wind is as good as anybody's," said Grandpa.

"Purty tricky, ain't she buddy?"

"No, sir; she jest won't go to mill, nor to meetin'—"

"That's one o' them nigger tales," said Grandpa; "they'll say anything. I drove her to mill myself, not long ago."

"Yes, sir, but you 'member she kicked the dashboard—"

"That was because the breeching broke. Any lively mule will do that."

"Look out, don't go too close to her heels," I put in, "for Solomon says she can kick a chaw terbacker out o' yer mouth and never 'sturb your front teeth."

"Purty high old kicker, eh, buddy? Takes a boy to understand hoss flesh an' their tricks."

"Well, the mule's all right," said Grandpa, "and as I told you, I'm not particular to swap."

I could see that he was dead set, now, and old Jin had dropped her head and looked like she'd lost every hope.

"Lemme see her teeth. Gad! the mule's sick right this minit," said Mr. Jernigan. "Phew! Done past the tooth age. Can't tell whether she's twenty or twenty-five."

"Oh, she's not old to hurt."

"No, no ; she won't never see twenty ag'in."

"Oh, she ain't that old."

"Git around here! Stir up, you old slug! Durned ef the animal ain't sick, right now. Better drench her. I mus' go ; good day."

"Hold on," said Grandpa, "the mule ain't sick. It's just her way. I like your hoss purty well, and I wouldn't mind givin' a little boot betwixt 'em."

"How much?"

"Oh, I dunno. Fifteen dollars."

"Fifteen durnations! Sebenty-five, or no trade."

"Oh, that's too much. Turn 'er loose, my son ; I don't much care to swap, nohow."

"What'll you give, now, and no jokin'? Fair's fair; I'll make it even fifty, fur you say you know my uncle Johnnie Jernigan, an' he's as good a man as ever lived, if I do say it, an' I'd like to be liber'l with uncle Johnnie's old friends."

"I'll give twenty-five, cash down."

"Oh, that ain't enough. It'll take ten dollars to cure that old rip o' the colic, or bots, or whatever it is she's got. I'll split the difference. Gimme forty dollars. I'll take your note fur the other fifteen. I know you're plum good."

Grandpa hesitated ; looked at the mule, then at the horse, then at Mr. Jernigan, then at me.

"I expect the boys will hate to part with the mule."

"I won't, I'm shore," said I, "'cause I haint forgot how she flung me—"

"She is gentle as a kitten, but they've pranked with her so much—"

"Flung you down, did she, buddy? Children know, I tell you. Well, wha'd ye say?"

"I b'leeve I'll do it. Come to the house, and we'll fix up the papers."

The trade was made, and Mr. Jernigan rode off in a fox trot, and just before he got out of hearing, he turned around and hollered back:

"I forgot to tell you that aire hoss is a little weak-eyed, but you won't mind a little thing like that."

At dinner time Solomon took a long look at the new horse.

"What do you think of him, Solomon?"

"Well, sah, ter tell yer de trufe, I'd rudder had old Jin, ole as she is, an' mean as she is, by fifty dollahs, dan dat ar ole hoss. W'y boss, dat hoss is done blowed up wid antimony, an' I b'lieve he's stringhalted, an', lemme see dem eyes! W'y, de Lawd er massy, ef dat ole hoss ain' stone blin'!"

Grandpa was terribly upset, but it was too late. He inquired after Mr. Jernigan, but the latter had stopped at Dekle's mill and traded the note, by shaving it, as they called it, and that was the last we ever heard of him.

A CHRISTMAS GUN.

Oh, I did want a Christmas gun so bad!

For weeks before Santa Claus had started on his rounds I was forever hanging around.

"Grandpa, how much do guns cost? Grandpa, can't I buy a Christmas gun? Grandpa, get me a gun."

The old gentleman must have got mighty tired of it, but I lived in hope if I died in despair.

In those days there were various ways of firing Christmas guns. Down at the shop Uncle Peter was able to make a pretty horrible explosion by spitting on the anvil, laying a piece of red hot iron on it and striking it a sharp blow with the big hammer.

I did not understand the reason for this at that time, but age and experience have informed me that it was the steam generated between the spittle and the hot iron. Now, if some other smart fellow would come along and explain to me just how comes steam to make a racket of that sort, I shall be a wiser if a sadder man.

I guess it is on the same principle of a popgun, but I swear I've never correctly understood the principle of a popgun, yet, I suppose, like the Grecian philosopher, that with a gun long enough and a pusher strong enough, a fellow could make a tumultuous noise in the world.

Then, there's another sort of a gun that was a rip-roarer, but it was rather expensive. That was to bore an inch auger hole in a tree, drive a peg in the hole with a groove in it for the train, and put powder in the hole. The way we fired it was by laying a nice little train of powder, putting some shavings and scraps of cotton on it, setting the shavings afire, and then retreating to a safe distance.

This was a pretty good sort of gun its own self, and it always reminded me of a story—a very funny story—that Grandpa used to tell us about an Irishman who had an aching tooth.

The Irishman, according to Grandpa's version, put powder in the tooth, touched fire to it and ran.

With the full white light of modern research, and the gigantic strides of scientific investigation, I am led to believe that the Irishman was a myth and the whole story a hoax, but I believed it then, and I was happy.

I knew General DeLoach once swinged his eyebrows off and loosened his front teeth, fixing a train for one of those explosions, but the General had wet his eyes so often that his vision was bad that day, so Grandpa said.

I did want a gun so bad.

I made life exceedingly interesting for Grandpa, on the gun question.

But Grandpa had some sense, and he waived the plea and I got no gun, although I got a good many other very nice things, among them a rag doll that affected my spirit sorely, for above all things I hated for anybody to suppose that I was not thoroughly masculine in all my preferences and predilections. I suppose I might have been a more useful citizen had I never changed my notions.

Old Christmas—you know that comes just twelve days after new Christmas—was a bright and beautiful day. On the night before I had sat on a log and shivered for half an to see if the sheep all got on their knees, as folks said they did, on old Christmas eve. That is a superstition, you know, and they further allege that the black ones get up on their legs and the white ones kneel on the ground. I don't know about that.

By sun up, and before the frost had melted from the

woodpile, a dozen big fat hogs were being scraped and scalded, and we were busy getting the sausage mill ready, and preparing for a hog-killing time.

Then when they were swung up, we boys stood around and claimed melts and bladders. We wanted the melts to broil and the bladders to blow up. I laid siege to the big blue barrow, and stood guard over him for three mortal hours, getting in everybody's way, and prancing around and cutting up generally, for fear of losing my rights.

It was royal fun to sharpen a twig and string a slice of melt on it and hang it over the glowing coals until it was done, and have it nicely seasoned with a pinch of salt.

I guess I could tackle one with undiminished gusto even unto this day. It was the lingering taint of the savage taste cropping out in our blood, and aided and abetted by the little negroes who were not far removed from the condition of their Hottentot ancestry, after all.

But after the feast was over we began on the bladders. It was a matter of personal pride with us to see who could blow up the biggest. We would blow and blow till our eyes stuck out like pot legs, and we would beat and bang them to make them stretch, and then we would brag about who had the biggest.

I blew up the biggest bladder I ever saw that day. It was the big blue barrow that furnished me the material, and I was awful proud of it.

Grandpa, he kept eyeing it, and I noticed that the old gent was in high good humor He held a conversation with Uncle Mose, and afterwards I could see that Uncle Mose was tickled half to death, and he would keep slipping, and sliding, and snickering around, and every now and then I would hear a half suppressed, " Jesus, Mar ster !' '

They were plotting my downfall, but I, in my childish innocence, went on my way rejoicing.

John Exom had given me an old ramshackle of a flint and steel gun, with only a remnant of stock, and no lock at all. The old thing was rusty, and choked up, and looked like it had been lost in time of the Revolution.

I wanted to get the thing cleaned out, but in spite of all the washing and rubbing and scrubbing I could do, it remained plugged up. When I asked Uncle Peter about it he said I'd have to burn the rust out of it, and while they were finishing up the hogs I embraced the opportunity to clean out my gun. I thrust the breach into the dying embers, and left it while I worked at the bladder.

While I was tying it up securely Grandpa came up to me, whetting the big butcher knife.

"Well, my boy, you've got a big Christmas gun now."

"Jesus, marster!" snickered Uncle mose, who was standing near, with his back to us.

"Yes, sir, I'm gwine to save it till next Christmas."

"Oh, no, I wouldn't do that. To-day's old Christmas, and that is just as good as new Christmas. Put it down and jump on it hard, now, and let us see what a gun you can shoot."

"Oh, no, sir, I can't," said I.

"Jesus, marster," whispered Uncle Mose under his breath.

"Why, yes you can. See here, do it this way,"

He laid the bladder down near a puddle that had been made in scalding the hogs. He fixed his feet carefully, and went on to explain: "Now, draw in a long breath, place your feet carefully, jump away up——"

"Slam—bang!—splash!"

"Jesus, mars-ter! Oh, I'm shot!" squealed Uncle Mose, as he jumped up and down and rubbed himself.

Everything was confusion, and as the smoke rose Grandpa picked himself up from the mudhole, with the remains of the bursted bladder clinging to his pants.

"What in the name of common sense is the matter, Moses? Was it loaded?"

Then he saw the old gun barrel smoking in front of the furnace, and the hot coals scattered all around, and he took in the situation.

Uncle Mose walked half bent longer than I did, though..

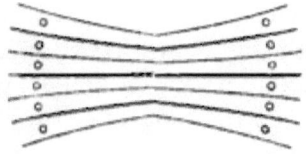

SNAKE BIT.

It makes my mouth water to think about that old sideboard.

Still, Grandpa was a sober man, strictly teetotal.

But that old sideboard that sat in the corner of the sitting room, up next the big fire-place.

A vision of that sideboard haunts me in my dreams.

And still, Grandpa was strictly temperate, and never touched a drop.

On that sideboard were two or three cut-glass decanters, with handles to them. One held good old-fashioned St. Croix rum—I doubt if you pronounce the word correctly, you who were born since the war. Another held Cognac, pure and simple, and a third—but these are prohibition times, and I will not tempt you further.

Often when I am pirooting around and doing sorter as I doggoned please, the memory of that sideboard comes up before me.

But Grandpa never drank—oh, no! buttermilk was good enough for him, and he drank it so persistently that his jaws hung down like wattles; and there was a sort of churn-dasher mellowness in his voice when he laughed.

But oh, my crackey! didn't those Thomasville lawyers love to visit that sideboard?

Grandpa would say:

"Boys"—always boys to him, for he never grew old himself nor imagined that any one else could be so silly— "Boys, there's sump'n to drink, there; jest he'p yourselves. You know I never drink, never liked the taste of it; but don't stand back on my account."

Men were not drunkards then like they are now; but twice a year those decanters had to be refilled, just after the spring term and just after the fall term of the big court, as we used to call it.

I suspect that the results of many a political issue have been dissolved and dissected by the aid of the impish spirits that danced around those decanters when the blaze crackled on the old brass fire-dogs, and was reflected in the prismatic carvings of those old decanters.

Grandpa kept the "sperrits" for snake bites, colics, rheumatic pains, and such like. That was why Uncle Mose was always colicky, and Popper Joe had twinges of rheumatism, and Yaller Jim was not a bit afraid of snakes.

One time, though, we all got into a scrape.

Old General DeLacy was very fond of Grandpa, and every now and then he would come around to pay us a visit. No regular time, mind you, but in the course of every six or eight months, for the General was a little like a comet in his peregrinations. He was sure to come, but you could never calculate just at what time.

He differed from a comet from the fact that he carried his tail in advance—that is, his fiery red nose answered for the tail; and it always preceded General DeLacy.

I have always had an intense antipathy for snakes. I was that way when a boy.

By the way, I have discovered several new varieties in my maturer years.

One fine April day, who should ride up to the gate but General DeLacy.

"Good mornin'!" he yelled, as he dismounted.

"'Light and come in," said Grandpa.

"How d'ye come on?" said the unceremonious visitor, as he pulled off the saddle and hung it on the fence.

"Jest toler'ble. Hitch yer critter, and I'll have him put up."

"Oh, he's all right," and he slipped off the bridle, gave the nag a cut with it, and, as the latter betook himself to the grassy fence jambs, his master sauntered up to the door.

They shook hands, and asked the news, and talked about half a dozen things in a breath, acting all the while in that agreeable, nonchalant, self-satisfied manner that betokened two gentlemen of immense knowledge and comprehensive information, to whom big topics were but as trifles when they met on equal ground.

I knew that the jig was up with me.

For the balance of that day there would be nothing but " Yazoo Frauds," " Missouri Compromises," " Whigs," " Democrats," and the dingnation bow-wows generally.

Set these two cronies to talking, and Gabriel might toot that trumpet till his heels flew up, and nothing short of catching each of them by the nape of the neck and bawling into their ears " Come on, you're wanted!" would disturb their composure.

I knew what I'd do. I'd go down about the fodder-house and hunt hens' nests. And if I got a chance, I'd slip up on General DeLacy's old horse and scare him into the hiccoughs.

I went sauntering down toward the lot. I took a lock of the fence on the old horse, and crept up right close and skeeted my hat at him.

I know you've seen horses act just as he did. He paid no earthly attention to the " skeet," but the next step of his left hind foot, he put it kerdab on my hat.

Just then he found some excellent grass, and he stood there, nipping, nipping, nipping; switching his tail from side to side, and every now and then a "phwoorff!" to blow the dust out of his nose.

And first one foot, then the other, up and down, stamp, stamp, stamp, and never moving from his tracks.

I clucked till my tongue stuck in the roof of my mouth, and I said " Git up, sir !" till my back ached ; and I finally had to get a stick and fetch him a cut to make him get off ; which he did so reluctantly that he ground my hat deeper in the dirt as he moved his old foot.

I wished that horse was dead. I did wish he was dead. Oh, how I wished he was dead, and I could see the carrion crows picking his bones !

" Rip !"

I had just reached the crib door when a big chicken-snake ran by me and under the crib. Back to the house I flew, crying :

" Grandpa ! Grandpa ! There's a big rattlesnake under the crib !"

" Rattlesnake ?" cried Grandpa.

" Rattlesnake ?" cried General DeLacy.

" Yes, and he is a whopper !"

In a twinkling we were out there and scouting around among the weeds and shucks.

" Ough-o-o ! I'm bit !" I yelled, as I felt something hit my leg as I passed the crib door.

They both ran to me, and sure enough there was a little speck of blood and a black and blue mark on my ankle.

" Got any licker ?" asked the General.

" Yes, at the house. Let's carry him there, quick. Ough ! I'm bit too," cried Grandpa, as he stepped a little too close to the door, and we heard the hiss of the reptile and the rustle of his coils as he gathered himself to strike again.

Oh, it was terrible ! I had always heard that even if a

11

person got well of a snake bite he'd have a snake hanging to his liver all his life.

Horrible thought !

Uncle Mose was the only negro about the place, and he and the General proceeded to doctor us.

"It warn't a rattlesnake," said the General, "for he didn't sing; but hit mought a'ben a pizen snake.   Even if hit war only a chicken snake hit mought make a bad sore. Gimme the licker."

" I don't think I'm bit much," said Grandpa, as he looked at his leg.   " Looks like a sorter glancin' lick."

" Here, take this," said the General, as he poured out a tumbler full of rum.

"No, no," said Grandpa, " I'd ruther be snake bit than to drink that."

"All right, I'll less'n the dose ;" and the General drank about half of it and said, "here, now, this ain't gwine to hurt you."

"No, give the boy a little; I won't drink it.   Bring me some tobacker, Moses; I'll fix a remedy."

I drank the balance of the liquor; and then they proceeded to moisten some broad pieces of tobacco and bind them to our wounds.

I was whimpering, and the General asked me if it hurt.

"Yes, it hurts bad."

"Pears to be crawlin' up your leg ?"

"Ye-es, sir."

"I knowed it.   A little more licker, Moses," and he poured out a brimming glass, by mistake, out of the brandy decanter.

"Humph!   I poured out too much, but I'll less'n it." said he as he drank about three-fourths of it, and gave me the balance.

I began to feel better.

"Moses, git a pole and go and see if you can stir up the snake. Call Jim to help you; he ain't a-scared of snakes. I'll be out there in a minit."

They made me go lie down, and the General bandaged my leg pretty tightly, and then he said:

"My stars! That war a worrisome job. I tell you, I've got nerves, or I could'nt astood what I did in the Injun war. I b'lieve I'll take a little toddy myself, now, to sorter straighten me up."

"All right, he'p yourself," said Grandpa, as he walked out to the water shelf.

The General poured out a tumbler full and drank it down, then he looked rather surprised and muttered:

"Humph! I made a mistake; that's whisky, and I wanted rum. I wonder which is the rum?" As he poured out a glass from another decanter, and drank it—"Why that 'ere's brandy. Ding the luck. I will find it," and he sampled the third glass, and smacked his lips and murmured with a grin:

"I yi! That's the truck. Now lay still, me boy, and we'll perceed to chase the sarpent."

The General walked out in a manner unnecessarily dignified, as I thought, and I lay right still, because my head felt funnier than my leg.

Uncle Mose told me the sequel afterwards.

"I tell yo', honey, de way I wus sca'ed dat day wus a caution. I t'ought dat you an' ol' Mars, bofe gwinter die.

"Me an' Jim, we went out da.' I tole Jim not ter go too closte; but he sich a imperdent nigger dat he say:

"'Yo' hush, Unc Mose, I gwinter have some er dat dram ef I hatter git bit twicet.'

"Sho' nuff, des 'bout dat time he walked closte ter de

fodder house do', an' zip!   He jump up so high"—measuring with his hand—"an' holler:

"'I'm bit! I'm—'

"'Cack! cack! cack!' de ole speckle hen lip out er de shucks an' des went er flyin' to'ards de house.

"'Dar's yo' snake,' I say.

"'No t'aint,' say Jim.

"'Yes it is,' say ol' Mars, who walk up des den.

"'Hooray fur Andy Jackson!' hollered de ol' Gin'l, es he come outen de lot.

"De ol' hen be'n hid in da', in de curises' place, an ol' Mars he tuck'n tored off dem rags off'n 'is laig, and he say :

"'Sich er pack er fool people I never seed in my bo'ned days.'

"'Aire yo' shore them ain't snake aiggs?' de Gin'l say.

"'Snake aiggs, yo' foot,' say ol' Mars', as he went walk'n off.

"De Gin'l look at me de funnies' an' he say:

"'Boy.'

"I say 'Suh!'

"He say, 'Ketch my hoss. I gotter go twenty mile dis day.'

"When I got de hoss ready de Gin'l git on de wrong side ter git up, an' I say:

"'Dis side, boss.'

"He say, 'Dat's all right. He's broke ter git on erry side.'

"Ol' Mars' say, 'Why, ain't ye gwinter stay tell a'ter dinner?'

"'Hain't got time, 'bleeged to you,' and he rid off in er weavin' way, sho nuff.

"Little piece down de road he met Jim.

"'Woa! Say, hain't you two boys twins?'

" ' Ain' no boy but des me, boss.'

" ' I know better. I see you bofe. Tell your master I'll give ten thousand dollars for you two boys. I jest be darned if I hain't been through two states, crossed six rivers, and fout in the war, but I never seed two boys as much alike as you aire. G'lang, Ball.' "

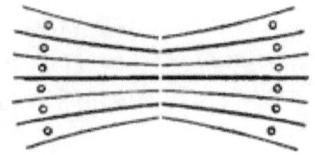

The preparatory lesson of every cracker boy's life is plowing a mule.

It might be all right to begin a business life by mixing up with a mule, but it is a mighty doubtful start for the kingdom of heaven.

Yea, by the beard of my fathers!

An average plantation mule used to be one-half unpardonable sin and the other half vanity and vexation of spirit.

Some of our most brilliant statesmen like to boast that they began life plowing a mule, but some of our most brilliant statesmen generally lie.

Ah, how well do I recall the days when I led forth a long-eared mule of angular build, and climbed up on a lock of the fence to get the hames over his neck.

As I leaned lovingly over to embrace the neck of the animated kicking-machine, it often occurred that he sprang aside, and I lost my balance, and came down among the sassafras sprouts and the dewberry vines.

And I would make use of expressions only found in certain sermons of modern manufacture; but they fell on unheeding ears.

And along about ten o'clock in the day, plowing in the new ground, where the soil was chiefly composed of black snakes and runner oak roots—talk about life! why, I have lived a hundred years in twelve short hours under such circumstances.

And, don't you know?—along about twelve o'clock, while Lazy Lawrence was dancing on the fence, that mule would keep turning his eye up to the sun and laying back

his ear that was next to the house, so as to hear the dinner-
horn's first toot.

Going down the row, the mule would keep the right ear
down ; coming up the row, the left.

And watching the sun all the time.

And just let that horn sound one note, and—

Halt!

Just as well to take the gear off, for the old cuss would
die rather than go another step.

Like some carpenters I used to know. They were
such sticklers for time that if one were driving a nail, and
had his hammer raised to strike the last lick, when the
clock struck he would lay the hammer down without
striking, and holler out—

"Time's up!"

Major Duckworth was a funny little man, with bow-
legs and the bearing of an orphan. He was so peculiar in
looks that irreverent men, who were so long-legged that
the little ends of their hearts were forked, used to call
him simply Major Duck, and frequently just—

"Hello, Duck."

The Major had many little tricks of conversation and
action that were more curious than captivating. He had
a way of sorter limping on one foot and scraping the other
along, and he would hitch up his breeches and say :

"Humph! be gad!"

Along a little piece further, hitch up, and—

"Humph! be gad!"

I think that was the reason why he always kept one of
his galluses slack, so as to have an excuse to hitch up his
breeches and—

"Humph! be gad!"

Major Duck owned a little sandy-haired mule that had

some as detestable ways as his master, and there was an everlasting conflict between them.

He also owned and controlled a meek and motherly wife, who pulled down the scales at a hundred and fifty. It did look like she could have managed Major Duck, but she couldn't, and the consequence was that all her aspirations were dwarfed.

One of the tricks of the mule was to stop to drink at every puddle, and another was to come to a dead halt at the fork of every road. If Major Duck wanted to go the road to mill, the mule wanted to go the road to meeting; and if Major Duck wanted to go to meeting, the mule would set his head on going to mill.

That mule was as wicked as Ahab, that tempted Israel to sin.

"Humph! be gad!" said the Major, "I'll l'arn ye some manners, ye brute. I'll fix a set o' gear fur ye that'll pester ye ef hit don't cyore ye. Humph! be gad!"

Down in the wire grass they didn't have any vehicles but those little two-wheeled carts with long shafts and a back band over the saddle, and the Major sat a-straddle of the mule, with a foot on either shaft, and drove.

There was nothing to prevent the cart tilting up if it got too heavy behind, and such a catastrophe was not infrequent.

The Major fixed some rawhide straps driven full of sharp nails that passed from the shoulders clean around the kicking end of the mule, and he fixed some lines that hung back in the cart. The mule would kick up when the Major tried to force him to go the proper course.

Every time the Major would hitch up, the mule would kick up until the dispute was settled.

"Humph! be gad, Betsy," said Major Duck to his wife,

"ye ain't had much injoyment, an' I perpose to let ye go to mill with me to-day an' ride in the cyart."

"I b'lieve I'd ruther stay at home."

"Ye had, had ye? Humph! be gad! Flew all to flinders when I couldn't carry ye to see yer mammy, in the heat of crap time. Now, ye've got to go. I've got business fur ye. Ye're jest like yer mammy, anyhow. Always do jest what ye hain't wanted to do."

The cart was loaded with a couple of corn sacks, and the mule was harnessed properly. As the Major arranged his compulsory harness tackle, and flung the lines into the cart, he remarked, with a hitch of his breeches:

"Humph, be gad! Bounce in, Betsy, an' when that ere mule stops an' don't wan't to go the right way—humph, be gad!—you jest tighten them ropes, an' when I say stick the dobbins to 'im, do you set back on them lines."

"Mr. Duckworth, you're agwine to cause that 'ere mule to do sump'n danger's an' I'm afeared to projick with your fixments. S'posen he were to run away, an' I were to be kilt? You'd be sorry then."

"Sorry? Humph! be gad! Hain't ther es good fish in the sea as ever were cotch out'n it? Humph! begad! I'd get me another un. But, don't you fret. This 'ere mule's too much like a jackass to run away. His game is to fight it out, an', humph! be gad! I'm agwine to give 'im a chance."

Down the road the little cart trundled, and the Major kept chuckling to himself—

"Humph! be gad!"

At the top of a long slope the roads forked. About half a mile ahead was a little muddy branch. Both of these points were among the battle grounds of the Major and the mule.

Just so. When they came to the forks of the road the mule stopped short.

"Humph! be gad! I'm agwine to give ye jest one chance, dadburn yer picter. Go 'long!"

The mule veered to the left and the Major pulled to the right.

" Go 'long, I say."

The mule sidled to the left.

" Humph, be gad! Shet yer eyes an' set back, an' stick the dobbins to 'im, Betsy."

Betsy set back and fetched a mighty pull.

There was a wild bray of surprise and pain, and that mule flung his heels into the air, and the wheels of that little cart only touched the high places, as they spun along the rooty road.

Betsy had set back a little too far, and she held to the lines to hold her position, and that drove the spikes in deeper.

Major Duck had to hold down the shafts with his feet and cling to the mule's neck with his hands, and away they went.

Bumpity, bumpity— "humph! be gad!" —bumpity, bump; bumpity, bump—"Do stop 'im Mr. Duckworth!"— Bumpity, bumpity—"humph! be gad!"

When they reached the foot of the slope the mule suddenly remembered that this was a halting station, and he stopped short.

The shock unsettled Betsy, and as she went over she raised the tackle till it caught the Major around the waist, and her weight threw the cart shafts up; and down they went, Betsy on the grass and the major in the mud over the mule's head.

Whoopee! He came out of that puddle, and he came a-cussing.

"Humph! be gad! Thought you'd kill me, did ye? Betsy, dadburn yer picter. I believe ye'd pizen me if ye got ha'f a chance. Git up f'om there. Yer not hurt. Humph! be gad!" and he hitched up his breeches that had been badly lacerated by the spikes.

"Oh, Mr. Duckworth, I knowed I'd be kilt. Oh, Lordy!"

"Git up f'om there, Betsy, I tell ye. Humph! be gad! I'll fix ye. Jest like yer ole mammy, make out like yer a'most kilt when ye hain't s'iled. Humph! be gad! Two bushels o'corn spilt an' the linch pin broke. All your durned fool actions!"

By that time he had got his breeches so they would stay up, and he walked around to where the mule was standing with his eyes half shut, resting and waiting for a renewal of hostilities.

"Humph! be gad! Hain't satisfied, aire ye? Ef my cyart weren't broke I'd stick the dobbins to ye ergin."

The mule opened one eye and glared at the Major, and sorter backed his ears and looked threatening.

The Major was too exhausted to accept the challenge. He threw himself on the ground, panting and foaming at the mouth. At last he feebly raised his clinched fist, and shaking it at the mule, he muttered:

"Humph! Be gad! You little, yaller, long-eared, crooked-legged, string-halted devil! Betsy's had enough, an, jest like er'ole mammy. But you—you—little wall-eyed cuss o' the earth; you git more and more like yer pappy every day!"

A SWARM OF BEES.

Grandpa got a notion into his head that bee-keeping was pleasant and profitable.

I didn't agree with him.

The only bee that I ever tried to keep was a bumble bee in a pumpkin blossom, and the old rascal ripped out at the side while I was holding the ends of the blossom to hear him "zoom," and he backed up against the side of my head in such a forcible way that I never forgot the experience.

But Grandpa knew he could manage bees.

He got hold of a gum with about a peck of these little black bees that smell rank when they get mad, and he set the gum against the palings, under the shade of the big sycamore that stood in the back yard.

Then he made me take a hoe and chop down the tea-weeds, so as to keep the toads and crickets from hiding there.

He tried to make me kill the old toad that persisted in sitting in front of the bee-gum and snapped up the workers as they came in from the fields. But folks had told me that if I killed a toad, my cow would die; so I just carried the toad off and dropped him into an old well, and told him to sink or swim, live or die.

Then he wasted several pounds of powder and shot trying to kill a little bit of a bee-martin that would fly at the shot and try to catch them, thinking they were bees. He never did kill the martin, but he said some ugly words about the martin, and the gun, and Ponchartrain for howling every time he took aim.

One day he told me he'd give me a dollar if I'd put an end to that martin, and Mr. Lewis told me that I could catch the martin if I'd put some salt on his tail; and I went around with a pocket full of salt for a whole week. One day I fell in the branch and the salt got wet and my breeches stiff, and skinned me all over; but I never could get close enough to the martin to conjure him.

When the plum trees shed their blossoms, and the little plums began to grow, the bees began to get restless, and late of an evening I could hear them growling and grumbling, and a big wad of them would stay outside till the dew fell on them.

I asked Grandpa if they wouldn't catch cold, but he told me to dry up, that boys like me couldn't understand such things.

"They are fixin' to swarm, and we'll have to watch 'em mighty close, my son. I reckon I had better not go to meetin' Sunday, for they mought swarm, and then agin they moughtn't. They giner'ly swarm when you're least expectin' it; and the Scripter says that it ain't no sin to pull an ox out'n the ditch on Sunday, and I 'spose bees aire as good as oxens."

That was his logic, and it suited me to a T.

Sunday was an ideal summer Sabbath. Just such a one as you see along about Easter, or a little after; when the soft blue skies are flecked with little white clouds that drift along like pleasure boats in a calm.

The air was full of fragrance and full of song.

The light winds rustled the tender leaves, and the old mocking bird sat among the peach tree boughs, and sang in a dreary sort of way, as if she were singing in her sleep.

The old dominicker stood on the fence and crowed. He would throw his head back and—

"Cuck—coo—cuck—coo—coo—oo—oo!"

And away down at popper Joe's house the old blue game would answer—

"Cuck-oo—cuck-oo-coo-oo-oo!"

And the old dominicker would hold his head sorter one-sided and listen, and then blaze away again.

The yellow hen laid an egg under the furnace, and came out cackling as if she had laid a nest full of ostrich eggs, with red and blue streaks on them. The yellow hen was as vain as a town girl with an Easter bonnet, and all about one little egg, that any hen could have laid.

Nobody at home but Grandpa and me.

He got a pillow and lay down on the back piazza to watch the bees, and I tried to get up a fight between old Pidy and Ponchartrain.

About eleven o'clock I heard a terrible buzzing at the bee gum, and I jumped up and ran to where I could see good, and it looked to me like there were about forty million bees darting around like they were crazy.

"O, Grandpa! the bees is a-swarmin'! the bees is a swarmin'!" I yelled, as I jumped up and down.

The old man sprang up and shaded his eyes with one hand and then shaded them with the other, for he had been hard and fast asleep.

"Well, they aire, by hoky!"

That was one of his cuss words.

"I seed 'em first, didn't I, Grandpa?"

"Yes—you're a smart boy, and you shall have the brindle calf for that."

"What aire you gwine to do?"

"O, we must make 'em pitch. Run, git two tin pans and sump'n to beat on 'em with. Run, quick, now."

I dashed into the kitchen and got two pans, and came

back ; and Grandpa took one and I took the other, and we raised a hullaballoo in about two minutes.

We beat, and we banged, and Ponchartrain followed us around and whined, and the old Pidy cat scaled up into the loft with her tail as big as a rolling pin, meowing and spitting at every jump.

The bees circled around, and circled around, and circled around ; getting higher and higher, and further away from the gum.

"Beat hard, my son, for they're atryin to run away," cried Grandpa, with the sweat streaming down his face ; and I just doubled myself up and nearly beat a hole in the big dish pan.

At last I saw a few of them light on a sycamore limb, and the rest all began to cluster around them ; and they flew slower and got thicker, and the first thing I knew there was a bunch of them hanging to the limb as big as a mule's head.

"Now we've got'em. All we've got to do is to git 'em in a gum. We've got to be mighty keerful, though, for they're a contrary set."

The gum had been made for several days in anticipation of their swarming, and we proceeded to get it ready.

"Grandpa, won't they sting us ? "

"Not if we ain't a-scared of 'em. If we let 'em know we're ascared of 'em they'll stick it to us, though."

We got the gum, and took some peachtree leaves and salt, and put them in water and bruised them, and we sprinkled the gum with water and set it on a table that we placed right under the bees.

"Now, I'll fix myself," said Grandpa, "for you know the Scripter says in time of peace prepare for war, and forewarned is forearmed."

I didn't know what the Scripture said about it, but if it
meant to rig a fellow up like Grandpa did himself that day,
I knew that I didn't understand the Scriptures.

He got a flour sack, and cut two little holes for his eyes
and a big one for his nose to breathe through, and he pulled
the sack over his head and tied it tight around his neck.
Then he put on his long linen coat and buttoned every one
of the big bright buttons, from the collar to the tail. He
then stuffed his breeches legs in his socks and tied them
tight around the ankles. He couldn't find any gloves that
were small enough, so he drew on a pair of woolen socks,
and made me tie the legs up around his wrists.

When he put on his big broad-brimmed hat, he looked
like the devil, or Robinson Crusoe, I couldn't decide which ;
and Ponchartrain growled and tucked his tail between his
legs as the old man came fanning out.

" Now, we must saw the limb off and let the bees down
right easy, and they'll go into the gum just so nice. I'll
saw the limb most off, and then you can finish it while I
ease 'em down."

I couldn't reach the limb, so I took a forked stick and
steadied it while Grandpa sawed. When he got it about
half in two he came and reached up and took hold of it, and
turning his back to the bee end of it, proceeded to direct
me.

" Saw easy, now, my son, and let it come down gently."

As he blinked at me through the peep-holes in that
sack, I snickered in spite of myself at the sight of that big,
red nose that looked like a pumpkin yam potato that the
wood-lice had been afoul of.

" Easy, now, it's a'most through."

My arms was so tired, for I had to sit astraddle of the
limb with my back against the tree, and reach out and saw

up and down. The old man braced himself firmly for the climax, and said :

"Steady, lad, we'll soon have 'em."

The nose grew redder every second, and damp splotches began to appear on the sack that covered his face. Ponchartrain sat under the edge of the piazza and looked on inquiringly.

Suddenly the old saw hung, and I fetched a surge, and snap ! went the limb.

The old man had miscalculated the weight of the bees, and as the limb parted so unexpectedly, the butt end flew up, and that whole dogoned half a bushel of bees overbalanced and struck him in the back, cur-rash!

Great balls of fire!

The air was full of the maddest bees that ever attacked a bald-headed man in the summer time.

They saw that red nose and they made for it.

Zip ! zip! zip!

Right and left, fore and aft, and sidewipe every second throwed in.

I climbed a few notches higher up among the sycamore limbs, and watched the fray.

Those hands with the socks on, went round and round like the paddles of a side-wheeler. Every lick they killed a dozen bees, but the swarm didn't miss them.

They got inside that linen coat, they forced their way into his breeches legs, and attacked flank and rear.

At last he made a break and tripped over the table, and down he went among the tea weeds. Ponchartrain thought now was the time to charge, and he sailed in, and every time a bee would pop him he'd take a fresh mouthful of the fallen monster.

After awhile Grandpa regained his feet and gave Pon-

12

chartrain a kick that would have paralyzed a mule, and tearing off his superfluous armor he made a dash for the branch.

I stayed up there until the bees collected and went zooming away toward the piny woods, and then I came down.

Just then Grandpa came in sight, but he didn't look near like he used to.

He and Ponchartrain had made up, and both of them had the biggest heads I ever saw.

And Grandpa's nose—phe-e-w !

He tried to talk to me, and got as mad as a wet hen because I couldn't understand him.

But about a week afterward, when I saw the bee-martin catching bees, I ran into the house and cried :

" Grandpa ! Grandpa ! Get your gun, that old martin's thest catchin' our bees."

"Let 'im alone, sonny. Let 'im catch 'em. Sich bees as them don't deserve no protection f'om me. Let 'im he.p himself to the bees, so far as I'm concerned."

Grandpa did hate to see animals treated cruelly.

He wouldn't even allow us to impose on the old spotted sow that was forever breaking into the potato patch, and when we tied knots in her tail to keep her from getting through the cracks, he made us catch her and untie them.

Then when we tied a turpentine saturated string to the cat's tail, set it on fire, and turned her loose, and she made a bee line for the big crib, the old gentleman came very near cowhiding us. I guess he would have done so had it not been for Yaller Jim, who headed the cat off and saved the big crib.

Grandpa was very humane, and would not let Ed Malloy cut Ponchartrain's ears when he was a puppy, so as to give him a watchful look ; and the dog had to go through life with flopped ears.

But there came a time when his excessive tenderness in regard to the animal kingdom brought him sorrow and dismay, and some melancholy experience.

Old man Horton had a few sheep, the worst sheep to butt folks that ever I saw in all my life. Perhaps our pranking with one old ram made him the chief of sinners in that line; but at any rate, he was the champion for butting.

Down by the river there was a high bluff with a second ledge just below the first one, and a nice little fringe of sparkleberry bushes all along its edge.

At the foot of the bluff there was a deep eddy, and on the other side of the channel a broad bar of snowy sand.

It was an elegant place to play, and many's the romp we had there in the olden time.

This bluff was a favorite sheep walk, and Horton's ram used to forage around among the sparkleberry bushes when the summer sun was high. Half a dozen of his boon companions were generally at his heels, and a high old time they had nipping the tender herbs in this cool and shady locality.

One day us boys hit upon a plan to get even with Horton's sheep, and the old bellicose ram in particular. We planned a stratagem that we felt sure would cool their martial spirits if the plot was skillfully executed.

We slipped around and got on the second ledge of the bluff where, by raising up, we could show ourselves, and then we could simply squat down and disappear like one of these "now-you-see-it-and-now-you-don't" kind of arrangements.

The sheep were feeding along above, and we could hear them as they'd "baa-aa-a" to each other and then "baa-oo-ea" back again.

We sat under the bank and snickered.

By and by they drew near unto us and we got ready fo' action.

One of the boys suddenly bobbed up and imitating the sheep said "baa-aa!" and made fighting motions.

One of those blear-eyed wethers accepted the challenge, and backing off a step or two lowered his head and came full tilt.

Lippity—lippity—lip! And just as he made his lunge the boy disappeared under the edge of the bank and a mighty splash in the pool below told the tale.

We laughed and danced for pure glee as we watched the sheep struggling in the water, and when he wiggled out on to the sand bar, forlorn and bedraggled, we fairly yelled with delight.

"Hey, there; what in the name of common sense aire you adoin' to Mr. Horton's sheep? Git out from here, you insignificant little rascals, or I'll cowhide you. Jest let me know of your being guilty of sich a thing ag'in ! "

It was Grandpa.

The old gentleman had slipped up on us unawares. He had his hog wallet thrown across his shoulders, and had been watching the whole proceedings.

It was pitiful to have to give the thing up at the interesting stage of the campaign, but we departed in obedience to the old gentleman's commands.

But we had an inkling that the old man wanted to try the sport, and as soon as we got a safe distance away, we paused to watch his maneuvers.

The sheep were on the bank bleating to their comrade, and after a cautious survey of his surroundings the old gentleman hung his wallet on a limb, and raising himself above the ledge, he took the big red handkerchief out of his hat, and shaking it in the direction of the old ram, he said :

" Baa-aa ! "

The old ram looked hard at him, and the old man ducked his head down under the edge of the bluff.

But the sheep was not on time and he raised his head up, and just as he did—

" Kervip !" come the old ram full tilt, and with a yell the old man turned a half summersault, and struck the water, and the old ram came down on top of him.

It looked like they dried up the channel for about twenty feet as they came down, and just such a churning up I never saw before.

We ran down to the edge of the water, whooping and yelling, and while one recovered the big red handkerchief, another fished out the hat.

Grandpa looked at the ram, and between his snufflings and splutterings he remarked—

"You old—hic—Philistine—ho-ck—I do wish you had a—squoi-ck—got drowned.   Sniff—any man that'll—snu-ff —keep sich unruly beasts—hic—'round him, ought to be-— sp-c-h-t—tuck up and dealt with!"

Then he waddled up the bank and got his wallet and marched off homewards, muttering and mumbling imprecations on the whole sheep tribe.

And for days afterwards a simple "baa-aa!" from one of the boys would set the old gentleman in a fidget.

BUSTLES AND THE BILLY GOAT.

In my childish innocence I used to wonder why they selected a he goat for the chief sinner of all the Hebrew nation. I used to hear Brother McCook speak of the scape goat that was turned into the wilderness, and I cogitated a great deal about it.

But I have learned by many experiences, that in rank as well as strength, the billy goat stands pre-eminent among all the beasts of the field ; and there was so much innate cussedness in his nature, that no wonder he was made an example of by the Jews.

But if their goats had have been like my uncle's goat, there would have been no use in turning him loose, for he would have died before he would have gone to the wilderness.

Jerusalem ! How I dreaded that goat. The old blear-eyed reprobate had a long yellowish beard, and was white behind and black before, and his horns twisted around like those you see in Bible pictures.

He generally fed in the fence jambs along the lane, so as to be in readiness to attack anybody whom he thought he could whip.

I used to sneak along on tiptoe, and the nearer I got to the house the lighter I got, and all of a sudden I would hear the ominous "ba-a !" and a vision of black and white wickedness on his hind feet would set me going.

Sometimes I would be assisted by a blow on the spot where my trousers were patched the most extensive ; and then again I would climb the gate post just as Billy struck its base with a shock that would loosen my teeth.

But there was little rest for the wicked, for that goat

could walk a three-cornered rail better than I could on the
ground, and there was no place except in the water where
I was safe from torment.

But Mr. Bustles, the jug-peddler, promised to teach the
old enemy some manners as well as sense.

Mr. Bustles was a man who had sandy beard and many
inventions. He looked somewhat like a goat, and he chewed
his tobacco so rapidly that the resemblance was made
more manifest.

He always used the words " Lord Geminy," to punctuate
his sentences.

One day I came in after a bloody engagement with Old
Billy, and after a hearty laugh at my expense he said :

"W'y, Lord Geminy, I kin fix that 'ere old ram in jist
a couple of minits, adzactly, by the Lord Geminy !"

"How, Mr. Bustles?"

"Ne'min'; jest git me a little homily pot, an' Lord
Geminy, we'll l'arn him a vallyble lessin by the Lord
Geminy! Git one 'bout big 'nough to fit my head, an,"
Lord Geminy, I'll make that 'ere kid wonder which end his
horns is hitched onto, by the Lord Geminy !"

We, the other boys and I, had to maneuver around a
good deal to secure the pot, for my lynx-eyed aunt put much
store by her kettles and her pots.

But we finally managed to slip it off, and down to the
lot we went, Mr. Bustles sauntering along humming :

> "Ole Dan Tucker, he got drunk,
> An' he fell in the fire an' he kicked up a chunk :
> An' a red-hot coal got in his sl oe ;
> An' Lord Geminee ! how the ashes flew !"

Under the crib stood Billy, chewing away, with a wicked
leer in his malicious eyes.

"Gimme the pot, an' hold my hat," said Mr. Bustles, "an' I'll see how it fits."

He carefully adjusted the pot, that fitted him like a cap, just covering his forehead, but leaving his eyes so he could wink at us as he remarked :

"See if the pot laigs p'ints straight for'ards, for by the Lord Geminy, I'm agwine to make that 'ere old Philistine feel like he's run ag'in a iron cuckle burr. Lord Geminy, s'pos'n he won't fight?"

"Oh, he'll fight," we all chimed in.

"All right. Here goes. He! he! he!" tittered Mr. Bustles, "Lord Geminy, won't I 'stonish that'ere ole animil!"

Then he walked up a little nearer the crib.

Billy wiggled his tail.

Mr. Bustles got down on his all-fours.

Billy blew his nose.

Mr. Bustles made a motion.

Billy raised his mane.

Mr. Bustles raised up and came down with a regular goat dare.

"Ba—a!" Rippity, rippity—bang!

Mr. Bustles turned a summersault backwards, and Billy trotted off with a sniff of disdain.

"Wa—augh!" Came a sepulchral voice as we climbed down off the fence, and Mr. Bustles scrambled to his feet, staggering, with the pot down over his ears.

"Lord Geminy, take it off!"

We grabbed the legs and pulled.

"Ou—w! Lord Geminy, my years!"

We took the legs and twisted the pot around.

"Stop! Lord Geminy, my whiskers!"

"What shall we do, then?"

"Lord Geminy, break the pot!"

"Might mash your head," said one.

"And the old lady would get us," said another.

"Lord Geminy, don't stop to argyfy. Break it easy; I'll pay fur the pot."

Finally we got the wood ax and an old hammer, and we made him lie down, and put the pot on the ax, and cracked it gently with the hammer until we got it off.

"By the Lord Geminy, mum," said he, as he explained it to the old lady, "thar's my waggin. Jest he'p yerse'f tell yer paid. Lord Geminy, ef you'll gimme that'ere goat ye mought have the whole layout. I jest want to cut his black throat f'om year to year, an' by the Lord Geminy I'll be happy!"

But Billy was standing on the comb of the carriage house, looking like Satan inventing a new sin, and Mr. Bustles drove off with his ears and nose covered with sweet gum salve.

THE JIMMERSON BULL.

There is something peculiar about the cow kind that I never could cipher out.

That is their pleasure to do just exactly different from what you desire them to do.

I know we had an old red-headed cow with one horn once, that was a tough case. In the spring and summer she would slip around and take a five-mile walk to find a low place where she could jump into the field.

And she didn't care much what was growing in the field, whether it was wheat or tares, she just would jump in or die.

Then again, when the fields were open in the fall, we couldn't keep her in the fattest pea-field that ever harbored a buck rabbit.

She would jump out or bust. She was one of the jumping kind, and came from a family of jumpers. She could crack her heels together and skim over a ten-rail fence so slick it would make your head swim.

And the old heifer would go along with the herd, and when they'd come to the cow-pen gap, and all the rest would jump over—only three rails high—she would fetch a long leap and flourish her tail around.

She just loved to jump.

The Jimmerson bull was another one of those cussed conglomerations of contrarieties.

He belonged to old man Jimmerson, who lived over across the creek, in the backwoods; but he had taken up on the plantation, and had been there so long he felt like he was boss of the hill.

Grandpa wouldn't molest the old villain because Jim-

merson was a Hardshell Baptist and Grandpa was a Hardshell Methodist, and he was afraid if he hurt that old bull
that Jimmerson would think he just did it for spite.

In the spring of the year the old bull would shed off
until he looked pretty passable, and then he'd put on airs
until some little three-year-old, with us boys to help, would
whip the daylights out of him, and then old Jimmerson
would get sullen and go moping around the plantation,
studying up some sort of mischief.

He got so after a while that he was spiteful, and when
he could get a chance he'd make us boys skedaddle.

I have been walking along singing

> " Jaybird settin' on a swingin' limb,
> An' he winked at me an' I winked at him."

when suddenly out of a patch of weeds would come old
Jimp.

" Oo-oo-oof!" and away I'd go, with old Jimp full tilt
behind me, with his heels cracking, and just as I'd skin up
a tree and get safe, he'd stop and go to feeding.

Then I'd have to sit up there ever so long, and he'd feed
around and watch me out of the corner of his red eye, and
every time I'd start to get down, he'd paw a little dirt and
throw it on his back, and shake his head and mutter,
" Oo-oo-oof!" as much as to say, " Just come down if you
dare!"

One of the old rascal's worst traits was breaking into
the field.

When he was young I guess he was a good jumper, but
he grew so clumsy that he couldn't jump, and then he'd
just walk up to the fence and deliberately tear it down with
his horns and walk in.

He dearly loved a fodder stack, for there he had nothing
to do but to stand in the shade and pull out wisp after

wisp, and select the choicest blades, and trample the rest under his feet.

We had to run after that old bull every day, and often of a night, and nobody could like such a bull as that, especially us boys ; and we hated him worse than poverty or sin.

We had been on the run for a week, one November trying to keep old Jimp from ruining a fodder stack, when at last Grandpa said :

"Boys, I'll fix that Jimmerson bull. I'll stop his fodder eatin'. I don't want to hurt the old villyun, for Mr. Jimmerson mought think I done it for spite ; but I'll fix him, now mind if I don't."

Grandpa had one of these old time single barrel shot guns, so small in the bore that you could load it with a big bullet and thick patching. She was sure fire, and I reckon Grandpa must have been a great shooter in his young days, for he was always bragging about what he could do if he had a mind to, with that old gun.

"Go load my gun," said he, "and put a plenty of powder, but instid o' shot put in a big load of coarse salt. I'll fix that bull so he'll let alone my fodder stack."

I ran off to load the gun, and I happened to think of just putting in one shot to get even with old Jimp. I knew it would take more than just one little buckshot to kill as big a bull as old Jimp, and I didn't much believe Grandpa could hit the old scamp, anyway.

Well, I brought out the gun, and Grandpa started down to the field, and Ponchartrain at his heels. Grandpa heard Ponch, and hollered to me to "come git this puppy and keep him back ; or I'll never git in gun shot o' that beast."

I ran out an collared Ponch and tied a string around his neck, but I wanted to see the fun so bad I couldn't resist following along at a distance.

Grandpa slipped along on the off side of the fodder stack till he got in about forty feet of it, and then he crawled to a stump to get a rest.

Ponchartrain began to whine, but I choked him.

I began to tremble with excitement as Grandpa pulled back the hammer.

Old Jimp stood with half closed eyes, chewing away, unsuspectingly.

Grandpa drew a long bead.

The sun glistened on the gun barrel.

Ponch wiggled and whined.

Old Jimp chewed his fodder.

I trembled.

Cherwhack!

The gun had missed fire, and I like to have yelled with excitement.

Grandpa cocked his gun.

Another bead.

Old Jimp stamped one foot—

" Bang ! "

" Bau-w-wr-r!" Old Jimp tumbled over and stuck his feet straight up. Ponchartrain broke loose and went yelping away toward the house.

Grandpa dropped the gun and drew a long breath as he placed his hands on his hips.

" Well, I'll be consarned! Them drotted boys! Them grains o' salt were too big!"

I had come up close behind and I snickered—

" Hey! You here? Ah-h! You little rascal. ¡You done that!" and I disappeared with a cornstalk in full pursuit.

DEACON DODDS.

The ugliest mortal that came to Salem church was Deacon Dodds.

He was a sight to look upon. He was of medium height, but so stoop-shouldered that it brought him down among the lower levels of humanity.

One eye looked up the chimney, while the other one was fixed on the pot, so that it was a proverb among us that Deacon Dodds would make a first-class cook.

He was not only cross-eyed, but he was cock-eyed, and blear-eyed, and his eyes were so close together that a gallinipper could sit straddle of the bridge of his nose and dabble a hind foot in the corner of each eye at the same time.

He was so bald that if he had had any beard it would have puzzled his nearest relations to have told which was the front side of his head.

And his ears stuck out like the fans of a windmill.

The free breeze of heaven had blown against his face until it was the color of a hogskin saddle after ten years' steady use, and his nose was like unto a reap hook with a rotten apple on the point of the blade.

But who shall describe his mouth?

It was like the overseer's wages, extending from ear to ear, and in its dark and cavernous depths two or three dilapidated yellow tusks remained, like memorial pillars that had been left when the cyclone struck it.

And he would sing or die. And no matter how many people were there Deacon Dodds was first to catch the tune, and above the rythmic swell of the voices of those who had some regard for time and meter, could be heard at intervals that discordant bray, like the cry of a wild ass of the desert among the palm branches.

I never did like Deacon Dodds. I don't know why, but some how I had a distaste for him. I used to wonder what kind of a looking cherubim Deacon Dodds would make if he should happen to slip in at the golden gate while St. Peter was not noticing.

And then again, I was a little bothered. If old Nick were to get him he wouldn't take him down there, because he was so ugly he'd put the fire out.

It used to tickle me when Grandpa would meet the Deacon and shake hands with him, and sorter squint one eye and then t'other eye, like a goose blinking at the sun, and it was:

"Howdy do, Brother Dodds," and "Toler'ble well, au' how do you do," and "I'm toler'ble, and how do you do," and right on, over and over again, while the Deacon appeared to be admiring the shape of Grandpa's hat with his right eye and taking the measure of his foot with the other.

And as his tongue would slosh around in that big empty mouth of his like a cat-fish in a puddle, I would think to myself:

"Old jockey, if I was as big as Grandpa, you wouldn't be any brother of mine!"

He had another quality more or less admirable. After he got through singing he always went to nodding, so he slept while others worshipped, and when he worshipped nobody else could sleep.

He would lean his bald head over the back of a bench, close his eyes and open his fly trap, and begin to snore the very minute the preacher got through reading his text, just as if he were away behind on sleep, and had determined to catch up, preacher or no preacher.

One day I occupied a seat just in the rear of Deacon Dodds. It was a still, sultry, summer day ; and scarcely had the last notes of the hymn died away when the Deacon settled himself for a regular snooze.

He had got down to business, and was sawing gourds for who laid the rails, when my attention was attracted by a big brindled grasshopper that was leisurely meandering along the window sill to find a cool and shady place.

The parson had taken his text in Revelations, where the prophet describes the monster that had so many horns, and created such consternation among the natives when he moved into the settlement.

My mind, ever active, instantly found a parallel between the monster and the brindled grasshopper. The more I thought about it, the more forcibly it struck me, and finally I reached forth and captured the grasshopper, and began to inspect him.

Just then I happened to glance at the Deacon's open mouth, and the thought struck me, "I wonder if there wouldn't be some more revelations if this gentleman was to saunter in there?"

The preacher was watching me, and I had to be sly.

I inched up right close to the Deacon who snored away.

The other brethen were all engrossed in the sermon, and the good sisters were blinking drowsily.

The parson was getting heated up, and as he took out his handkerchief to wipe away the perspiration, I got right close to the Deacon.

Slowly and cautiously I eased my hand forward.

Just then the parson hit his beast an imaginary lick betwixt the eyes with a bang of the fist by the way of emphasis.

A little nearer I reached.

13

The Deacon snored.

Nearer and nearer.

The beast was approaching perdition.

A quick, deft movement, and—Great Jewhilikins!

The brindled grasshopper disappeared, but if ever you saw a circus it was there.

Spitting and spluttering, coughing and struggling, the Deacon reared up in his seat and his eyes stood out on stems as he heaved and hawked, and hawked and heaved, all the time making the most ungodly grimaces that mortal man ever was guilty of.

The parson turned red in the face, reached for the water pitcher and almost broke down completely.

The sisters started from their seats with many a " Lord a' mercy ! " and the brethren came forward to assist Brother Dodds, who was evidently in a fit.

" Wa—a—k ! Sq—sq—ack ! scuff—ff ! swish—s—sh ! oo—oo—o—aick ! " went he like a bursted locomotive boiler as he walked half bent down the aisle toward the door.

Just as he reached the steps the brindled grasshopper fell, a limp and shapeless mass of legs and horns, at his feet.

With eyes starting from their sockets and trembling from head to foot he stammered :

" Th—th—ank the L—L—Lord ! "

" Do you feel any better, Brother Dodds ? "

" Y—Y—Yes, but it w—w—wus a p—p—pow'ful n— narrer 's—scape. D—you—r—reckin hit's a t—t—tokin of the b—b—beast ? "

THE WITCHES.

The wild winds of December had chanted the last stave of their noisy requiem over the chilly couch of the dying year, and now there were only occasional gusts, and half-uttered sighs among the drooping boughs of the pine trees. The last muddy shred of wintry cloud followed in the wake of the wintry sun when he sank behind the western ridges, and one by one the shining stars peeped from the dark firmament.

First came the twinkling Pleiades on their mournful quest, traversing once more the heavenly plain as though they still had hopes that their tireless search, that had continued through all the long centuries of the past, might be at last rewarded. Aldebaran followed, his bloodshot eye glowing with a deeper intensity through the frosty atmosphere. Stalwart Orion climbed the spangled steps as he had done often and again from time immemorial. Away toward the north pole, silent and alone, sat the pale North Star, heaven's unchangeable beacon, on whose cold glitter the eyes of earth's millions gaze in awe and wonder. Another year added to the unnumbered ones that lay finished, sealed and filed away in the immeasurable vaults of the ages.

And yet the world moved on. Not a moment's stop; the everlasting wheels turned around in the same old grooves, and man was left without a moment for contemplation.

"To-morrow's New Year's," said I, as I entered Uncle Mentor's cabin.

"Yes, an' if yo' don' do er good day's wo'k termorrer, yo' ain' gwin do notin' de whole year. I've al'ers hearn say dat if you fool about on de fus' day uv de year, yo' des sho' to keep it up tel that year go out. Now, my ole marstah, wa't live way back'n ole Keerlina, he al'ers wo'ked ha'd on dat day, 'case 'e say dat's de way ter make er good crap. Dese days folks des goes or traips'n erround f'om pos' ter piller lack dey don' ca' w'edder dey make any crap er no."

All this time the old man was busy making brooms.

He had a big bundle of long broom sedges lying by, and he would take up a handful of it, and with an old table fork he would comb it out until every straw stood up correctly, and the little blades and frazzles were all stripped off. Then he would cut the butts off the straw nice and even, and beginning with a long white oak split, he would wrap and weave the straw into a nice broom. In some way the white oak didn't work well, and with a jerk he muttered:

"Now, wat's de mattah wid dis split? Look lack it 'us bewitched."

"Bewitched, how?" said I.

"Oh, des conju'ed by dem ol' witches. You know dem ol' witches, dey has heap to do wid brooms. Dey rides broom han'les w'en dey goes off ter dey frolics. Dat's de reason folks orter use dis yere so'ter broom, an' not tinker wid dem sto' boughten brooms, 'case boughten ones is got long han'les, an' de ol' witches do luf to ride 'em."

"How can they make 'em go?" I asked, growing interested.

"Laws a me! Don' ax me nuthin' bout how dey does. S'pose I ben projeckin' erroun' wid dem ol' ash cats? No, sah! All I know's w'at I hear udder folks say. One time dey wus er boy, an' 'e al'ers wantin' ter know sump'n' 'bout witches. 'E kep' on axin' 'e gra'ma 'bout 'em twel at las' she say, she did, 'Jacky, honey, ef yo' wanter know sump'n' 'bout'n dem witches yo' des watch yo' aun' Sookey, she's one er dem witches, she is, an' evah week on Friday night she goes off ter de witches' meetin'ouse, and she dances wid 'em twel de clock struck twelve. Now min' w'at I tell yo', w'en yo' goes to dey house, yo' uns do des lake dey do. Ef yo' call de name uv de good Lo'd wiles yo' in dar, yo' gwine ter git in a scrape, sho.'

" So Jack, 'e went, 'e did, 'n 'e watch 'e auntie all Friday evenin'. 'Long 'bout dus' 'e see she git'n' mighty res'less, an' de fus'es fing 'e know she ha'f way ter de branch So 'e lit out 'n 'e hid in some bushes, an' 'e see 'e auntie come down ter er holler bla'gum, and dar wus er billy goat tied lack er hoss ter er swingin' limb. She made er roun' ma'k, she did, an' she made er cur'us ma'k wid er broom' stick w'at she had. She wa'k all erroun', so, an' den she jumped frough dat ring free times, an' she lip erstraddle uv de billy goat, an' she say, ' Up, Jack, an' erbout ! ' an' de billy goat des sailed off in de air.

" Jack felt mighty cur'us 'bout sich perceedin's, an' fus' fing 'e know, 'blip' ! come de billy goat ergin, an 'e hitch 'ese'f ter de same ol' swinging limb. 'Twa'nt long fo' er nudder one uv de neighbo' omerns come an' done des de same way. Dey kep' er comin' twel eight uv 'em come an gone.

" Jack knowed dat dey was only one mo', so 'e 'cided 'e'd tek er cider, an' so 'e went frough dem same monkey motions, an' w'en 'e say 'up, Jack, an' erbout,' de billy goat des na't'ally siz frough de air, an' 'e come down 'ker vlip ! ' frough de chimley uv er ol' house what Jack done heah folks say was ha'nted.

" Dey wus all dem ol' omerns tu'ned ter witches. An' dey des er jumpin' up'n' down, an' singin' songs, an' flingin' fox fier 'bout, an' er laughin', an' er havin' er reg'ler jubilee. Dey look so'ter skantwise at Jack, w'en 'e fus' come in, but 'e done changed inter er reg'lar ol' witch, an' dey 'cided at las' dat 'e wus de yodder ole witch. Den Jack 'e feel so good dat 'e commence ter whoop an' holler 'n' dance erroun, an' 'e nevah could jump es high in 'e life 'fo' dat time, an' 'e wus er likin' de fun.

"Dey swing all erroun, dey did, an' dey dance up'n' down de flo', an' dey skin de cat on de jistes, an' dey holler 'n' squall, an' fling summersets, an' I tell yo' w'at dey wus enjoyin' a big ol' time.

"A'ter er wiles Jack got so happy dat 'e say, 'God! ain' we havin' fun!' An', gentlemens, time 'e got de wo'd out 'n' 'e mouf dem witches all gone lack er flash, an' de place all da'k es pitch in dar.

"Jack, 'e fumble erroun twel 'e fin' de old billy goat, 'n' 'e say, 'up Jack 'n' erbout!' De ole billy goat 'e lif up an 'e des bobble erroun' 'mongst de rafters. Now, yo' know, Jack 'e done fo'got. 'E orter say 'up, Jack, an' out,' w'en 'e wanter git out; an' a'ter erw'ile de billy goat come down on de flo'.' Den Jack 'e study an' study w'at 'e gwine do. Las' 'e try erg'in, an' de goat des butt 'e head erround 'mong de rafters, an' 'e look lack 'e didn' know de way out'n dar.

"Las' 'e fink to 'e self, 'well, I don' wanter go, but I wanter git out, so' 'e jump straddle uv de billy goat, an' des es 'e did er mon'srous big ole black cat say 'meow-ow-ow!' up'n de top er de house, an 'e look up an' dar set de ole cat wid 'e eyes des lack coal er fier, an' 'e had er big chunk er fox fier in 'e paws, an' 'e flung it at Jack, an' 'e bow up 'e back 'n' 'e look vigus, an' 'e say, 'me—ow—ow! Shtoof! shtoop!' An' Jack 'us sca'd mos' ter deaf. Den 'e heah er nudder one growl, an' 'e look on udder side de house, an' dar wus er nudder big black cat, an' peah lack de whole place full uv dem sca'ful lookin' beas'es. An' Jack 'e up 'n' say, 'e did. 'Great God! wey all dem cats come f'om?' No soonah 'e say dat we'n 'zip,' dey all gone.

"Den 'e heah sump'n say 'siz-z!' an' 'e look an' dar was er gre't big snake quiled up on de jist, an' w'en 'e'd lick out 'e' tongue er stream er dat fox-fier des come 'er sizzin' at 'im, an' den mo' snakes comes twel de whole house full er snakes. Den 'e got to trim'lin' all over, an' 'e say, 'My God! ain' dis er snaky place?' No soonah 'e say dat den, 'spang'! de snakes all gone.

"Den 'e say quick, fo' any have time to come back, 'e say, 'e did: 'Up, Jack, 'n' out!' An' de billy goat des flew up de chimley, an' 'e heah sump'n' squeal an' 'e look erroun', an' dar come er whole drove er gre't big ole co'n owls right a'ter 'im, an' dey pop dey bills, an' some times dey take 'im zip er side 'e head, an' 'e holler, 'My God! don' hit er fellah in de eye!' An' den dey all gone fo' yo' can' can say Jack Robinson.

"Down come de billy goat at de ol' bla'gum tree, an' dar stood all dem witches, an' dey tuck a'ter 'im, an' 'e run des 'es ha'd es 'e kin split, an' 'e beat dem witches es pant-in' es dey run, and des es one uv 'em was reachin' out ter ketch Jack de ol' clock in de big house say 'ding, ding, ding, ding, ding, ding, ding, ding, ding, ding, ding, ding,' twelve times. Dat was all dat save Jack, and wen 'e woke up nex' morning, 'e had'n' got ovah 'e sca' twel den.

"W'en 'e come ter breck'us 'e look mighty po'ly, an' 'e gra'ma says 'Jack w'at de matter wid yo?' Den 'e says fo' 'e t'ought anything 'bout it: 'Up, Jack, an' out,' an' genter-mens, 'e an' Aunt Sookey was at de table, 'en she fell out er de cheer, an' had er fit, right dar. Dis sca'ed 'e gra'ma nearly to deaf, an' she lack ter whip de boy, an' 'e say, 'granny, I won' do so no mo', an' she let 'im off. But I tell yo', dat boy did'n' have not'in' mo' ter do wid de witches."